The Bait

Also from C. W. Gortner

The First Actress
The Romanov Empress
Marlene
The Vatican Princess
Mademoiselle Chanel
The Queen's Vow
The Confessions of Catherine De Medici
The Last Queen
The Tudor Secret
The Tudor Conspiracy
The Tudor Vendetta

M.J. Rose and C. W. Gortner
The Steal
The Bait

Also from M.J. Rose

The Last Tiara
Cartier's Hope
Tiffany Blues
The Library of Light and Shadow
The Secret Language of Stones
The Witch of Painted Sorrows
The Collector of Dying Breaths
The Seduction of Victor H.
The Book of Lost Fragrances
The Hypnotist
The Memoirist
The Reincarnationist
Lip Service
In Fidelity
Flesh Tones
Sheet Music
The Halo Effect
The Delilah Complex
The Venus Fix
Lying in Bed

M.J. Rose and Steve Berry
The Museum of Mysteries
The Lake of Learning
The House of Long Ago
The End of Forever

M.J. Rose and C. W. Gortner
The Steal
The Bait

M.J. Rose and Randy Susan Meyers
The Fashion Orphans

The Bait

C.W. GORTNER
and
M.J. ROSE

The Bait
By C. W. Gortner and M.J. Rose

Copyright 2022 C. W. Gortner and M.J. Rose
ISBN: 978-1-952457-66-1

Published by Blue Box Press, an imprint of Evil Eye Concepts, Incorporated

Prologue

Jerome

There are a lot of perks to having a rich girlfriend.

I've never thought about it before, how easy money makes things. In my line of work, it isn't something I tend to think about because I never have any extra dough to throw around. Sure, I know how rich people live. It's my job to know and deal with their dismay when their perfect lives are upended. I also know, more or less, how much they spend on stuff I've never considered essential. I mean, who really wants to eat a bunch of tiny, salty, black fish eggs from Russia at four hundred dollars a serving? A rich person, that's who. Not because it tastes great, but because they can. I suppose when you have so much money you don't know what to do with it, Russian fish eggs can taste pretty damn delicious.

I still don't get that part.

But the rest of it? I'm starting to understand. The private plane, for one, and the five-star hotels with fancy monikers and white-glove service. Suites bigger than any apartment I've rented—which isn't saying much, considering my London flat is about the size of Ania's walk-in closet. She insists on fresh flowers and always gets them, says they inspire her creativity—not that she's doing much designing these days. Still, fresh flowers are her rule.

And the other stuff: the fancy boutiques that don't look like they actually sell anything—all polished glass, creamy leather, and pristine displays with a single handbag, like a museum. No price tags. No money exchanged. It's all *on account*, or so Ania tells me. The restaurants where a phone call instantly opens her preferred table, no matter if it's a crowded Saturday night. Trust me, it's something to see. So is the astonished look on the maître d's face—she taught me that word after I called him "the host guy"—when she walks in with me at her side. That look is worth the prices not listed on the menu. I never knew there were places you could eat a steak and have no idea what it costs.

To her, it's normal, even if she can tell it's not normal to me. That it makes me uncomfortable. She says, "It's what money is for." Because that's how she sees it. She's never known differently, so I can't really blame her.

So, yeah. A lot of perks. For me, it's like hiding out in first class and wondering when I'll get caught. I keep thinking…anytime now, they'll come around to check my ticket and find out I only paid for steerage.

I'd say it's wonderful. And, mostly, it is. How many guys can say the same? Not many, I'll bet. I sure never thought I'd be one of them. Not in a million years.

Except for two things.

She doesn't like me calling her my girlfriend.

And we're both thieves.

Los Angeles Daily News. December 15, 1958

Oh, my dovelies. Do I have news for you! Yes, NEWS. Yours truly, Tattle-Dove, has just learned we're off to Venice. No, not the neighborhood. Italy, darlings. To Carnival, no less. You haven't heard of it? Where on earth have you been hiding? It's a grand tradition in those foreign parts, where everyone who's anyone—and quite a few who wish they were—congregate to soak up the grandeur, gondolas, pasta, and all that jazz.

And I'm going there, too. To report on the social event of the season. What you might call the *launch* of the season. Yes, dovelies. I've been invited to the annual costume gala of *Contessa di Maglione*, who some of you may remember as Julie Kimbell, leggy star of such epics as *Blood in the Arena* and *The Emperor's Favorite*. Well, she's a countess now, didn't you know? If you missed her wedding coverage, I assume you've been hiding under a rock. And her ball is very exclusive, so much so that only those who're definitely somebody get invited. So, wish me bon voyage. And stay tuned to this page. I'm sure we'll have plenty to tattle about when I get back. Ta-ta for now! Or should that be, *ciao*?

Chapter 1

Jerome

"Stop fidgeting," Ania hisses under her breath. "You're supposed to be enjoying this." Even as she scolds me, her smile is serene, though her cat eyes glitter like shards under her mask.

"I told you, it's too tight." I tug again at the starched, upright collar of the impossible getup she insisted I wear. White tie, she calls it. More like noose-tied-around-my-neck. "And I'm not a paying member of your high-society club. In case you've forgotten."

"How can I, if you never stop reminding me?" she replies. "We've been planning this for nearly a year. We have this one chance, so let's get on with it. Okay?"

I start to grimace. At another glare from her, I force my expression into some semblance of whoever-that-guy-is-with-Ania-Thorne-ought-to-look-like. It's quite the occasion, after all. The event of the year. Ania even airily introduced me as her *friend*—a euphemism not lost on our hostess, Contessa di Maglione, whose annual costume ball for the Venetian Carnival is, at least according to those who care, the only place to be.

I'd thought being stared at by a maître d was funny until I saw the way the countess raked her gaze up and down me. As if I were an unexpected course for her buffet.

"Did you see the way she looked at you?" Ania now whispers, a flute of champagne in one hand as she twines her other hand around my arm. It's an overt display of affection with nothing affectionate about it. "She took the bait. Look at her, the queen of the ball. Like Marie Antoinette. Before Marie lost her head. And her diamonds."

"Ouch." I flex my arm, squeezing her hand. "I thought you liked her."

"*Like* her?" She takes a sip from her flute, nodding at a passing couple in some kind of historical outfit that makes them look like Chinese pagodas. "I never said that."

"But she's a client—" I start to say.

"A *former* client." Ania slips her hand from my arm to my neck and wiggles her finger under my collar to relieve the bowtie's stranglehold on my windpipe. "Better?"

I suck in air. "Thanks." I pause, wishing I could smoke. You'd think smoking would be permitted at a party like this, all the canapes and champagne, everyone dressed like Halloween. It isn't. The invitation specifically forbade it. Maybe all these hoopskirts and powdered wigs are highly flammable.

"Are you sure about this?" I shove my hands into my trouser pockets and then take them out at her exasperated look. "Was a client, is still a client."

Her voice takes on an edge I'm becoming all too familiar with. "She never bought any of my pieces. She left us after my father—" She cuts herself short. "A former starlet. Her claim to fame was a series of tawdry gladiator movies. Then she got married to money. After that, it was contessa and Cartier."

"Guess she misses the red carpet, huh? I mean, look at this circus." I try to sound jaded but only manage to come across as silly, even to myself.

I get a jab in my ribs from her elbow for it. "You read her file, didn't you?"

"Yeah."

"And you saw that necklace she's wearing."

"I did. Quite the loot, even with a defective clasp."

"Then why the doubts?" She finishes her champagne; her face smooth as glass as she surveys the party. "She'll do as I said. Leave the necklace on her nightstand or in an unlocked safe before the dancing starts. Because she's afraid to lose it. We offered to repair the clasp free of charge. It's in her file. We always offer the service to past and present clients."

"But she refused to bring it in for repairs. Or to exchange it."

"She's a bad actress. She's not stupid. She married because her career was going nowhere, and her husband prefers to spend all his time at Lake Garda, so she can run about spending his money. That yellow diamond necklace is vintage Thorne. One of my father's earliest pieces. She wasn't about to let us get our hands on it. How could she? In her mind, we might never give it back."

"Right." I know all of this. I read the file. I studied it, in fact.

Julie Kimbell, born Anna-May Kimsky in Queens, made her way to Hollywood, searching for the spotlight like a thousand other pretty nobodies. As the story goes—if you can believe Hollywood stories—an agent on the lookout for a new pair of legs discovered her selling stockings in a Wiltshire department store. She scored her first part after a screen test. Or a casting-couch test. Whatever the case, with a thousand other pretty nobodies chomping at her heels, once it became clear that Julie Kimbell would never amount to more than Roman concubines pining for heroic gladiators, played by male stars earning three times her salary, she parlayed those legs into a proposal from an infatuated Italian count twice her age, with enough cash to satisfy her hunger for the high life. Goodbye, Hollywood. Hello, palazzo in Venice, coveted annual ball, and vintage Thorne.

It took Ania months to settle on her as our target. She combed through the files Luke sent like I would investigate a burglary scene. With Mr. Cologne—aka Luke Westerly—in charge at Thorne & Company, appointed by Ania as her co-director so she could take an unspecified leave of absence, we gained access without raising alarm bells with the board, still on high alert since the incident in Cannes. I have to admit, Mr. Cologne is a cool customer. He didn't bat an eye. He survived our encounter with the Leopard in Paris with a slight scar on his well-moisturized forehead. And when Ania relayed our plan, he drawled, "Naturally, darling. Anything for you. Do have a care, whatever you're up to."

She didn't explain what she was up to, but the bump in his rank and pay must have done the trick. Because *anything* for her turned out to be the records of Virgil Thorne's past sales, specifically pieces not returned upon request for inclusion in the company archives. Other clients, including movie stars far more famous than Julie Kimbell, gladly accepted current market value for their piece or commensurate exchange for one of

Ania's current designs. Not Julie. She replied that she couldn't possibly part with her beloved Thorne necklace, an engagement gift from her senile count.

Guess she's about to part with it now.

Ania claimed it would be the easiest piece to swipe. Julie never hires security for her balls. She thinks it's déclassé, a word I had to look up. I'm not surprised. Rich people never think they need security until they do; by then, it's usually too late. And Anna-May Kimsky wasn't born to any of this. She slept her way to it, so she still has a starlet's attitude. To her, all that matters is how it looks. Not how safe it might be.

"It's going to be fine." Ania breaks into my thoughts. "Do you see anything we should be concerned about?"

"Except for the hundred or so guests? Nah. Piece of cake. By the way, isn't that why they stole Marie Antoinette's diamonds? Because she ate too much cake?'"

"Honestly." She draws back her slim shoulders. "Stay here. I need to mingle."

As I watch her melt into the crowd, her bare back a white seam under the scoop of her clingy black dress, I feel heat in my groin. She still takes my breath away, damnit. From the moment I first met her in the hotel in Cannes after the Leopard made off with her collection, she's had this hold on me like a leash.

Not that I'll admit it. I keep telling myself I'm doing this because she was going to do it anyway. Because there was no stopping her after her father played her for a fool. Because if I didn't help her, she would end up in a heap of trouble—and likely in a jail cell.

That's what I keep telling myself. Even if I don't like it.

I wanted to be the one to do it. Ania refused, countering that Julie would zero in on me, the new man in town—which I wasn't sure I should take as a compliment. I had to be the distraction. While I kept the target busy, she'd do the job.

Still, as I scan the area again, I wonder at my willingness to go along. I don't spot anything suspicious. No obstacles on that immense marble staircase. No goons lurking in the background, keeping an eye on the merchandise. Just hired staff, circulating platters of champagne and canapes, candlelight wavering in the mirrors framing the walls, violin music wafting from the ballroom, and the babble of people with too much of everything, indulging in too much of everything. The event of the season.

Who would think anything could go wrong?

I focus on the layout. I managed to unearth the floorplan in the city's moldering Accademia, after charming a dumpy librarian with my crappy Italian and bold American smile. Turns out the palazzo is historic, like everything else in Venice. Used to belong to a doge's advisor, passed down to his descendants, the last of whom is Julie's count. The living quarters are upstairs, all with names starting with *piano*, which caused me some confusion until Ania explained it's the Italian term for *floor*, not the instrument. Off-limits to guests. The ball is held on the first level, in a former area right above the canal. The moisture-damaged walls were knocked down, the old flooring dug up. Everything renovated to modern standards by the obliging count for his trophy Hollywood wife.

Ania has to get up that staircase, slip into the piano-whatever Julie's bedroom is, steal the necklace Julie will allegedly leave, then make her way back down to the party. Without being seen.

Like I said, I don't like it.

I return my gaze to the crowd, trying to catch sight of Ania. When I do, I'm startled to find her with a hand on her hip as a tall, well-built man with a dark blond crewcut, an impressive jawline, and a velvet tuxedo whispers in her ear.

Something lodges in my chest. An intimacy there…the way she tilts her head to him as if to soak in his confidence. Not like with Luke Westerly. Not familial.

"Pretty spectacular, isn't she?"

I jolt at the voice behind me, turning to find myself looking down into inquisitive sea-foam eyes that are a little too direct. A mop of reddish curls. Pert nose with a smattering of freckles. Pert lips, too, if a bit overboard on the lipstick. Pretty, if you like that sort of look.

"What?" I say hoarsely.

"Your…" A slight frown. "Well, I'm not sure. Who is she to you, exactly?"

"She's Ania Thorne." I take a step back to better take the person in. Lavish green gown like a Southern belle, froths of lace to show off her bared shoulders, and an emerald choker. Real stones but muddy. Inferior. I give myself a pat on the back for noticing. My time with Ania hasn't gone to waste. I can now spot quality at a glance, when before I required a professional jeweler. But that's who Ania is, right? A professional.

And I get the feeling this girl knows it.

Except she's not really a girl. The first impression is of girlish eagerness, but closer inspection reveals faint lines cradling the too-red mouth. Smile lines, too.

A woman. Probably in her early thirties.

She smiles as if she can read my thoughts. "I know who she is. Who doesn't? That wasn't my question, handsome."

"She's my friend," I say, echoing Ania's introduction of me.

"American. I thought so. You look it."

"Do I?"

A burst of laughter. "You do. So do I. All the way from California." She thrusts out her hand. "Lauren Segal. Pleased to meet you, Mr...?"

I shake her hand. "All the way from California." I force out a smile, ignoring her attempt to get my name. "What are you doing in Venice?"

"Same as you, I suppose. Taking in the scenery." Her eyes shift to Ania, still with her back to us. Still in intimate conversation with Mr. Impressive Jaw. "Mm. Hugh Lockling. Now, there's an item."

I have to physically stop myself from looking around. Then she returns her stare to me with the precision of a missile. "The aviation heir? Lockling Enterprises?"

I shrug.

"Really? Never heard of him? He's her ex-fiancé."

That's a direct punch to my stomach. "Is he?"

"Oh, sure. Quite the pair, five or six years ago. Engaged to be married." She leans to me as he's leaning to Ania, only Lauren's gesture is conspiratorial, two outsiders sharing a secret. "Broke up over something. Never spoke about it in public, but everyone had their suspicions."

"Oh?" I almost recoil from her.

"Of course. She's famous, isn't she? So is Hugh Lockling. And then there's her father. Everyone knows Virgil Thorne was preparing her to run the business once he retired. It turned out to be earlier than expected, but still. Maybe he didn't want his life's work and his only daughter devoured by the Lockling maw."

"Maw?" I think about the jaw, and now I really want to turn around.

She laughs. It's warm. Spontaneous. As if she laughs a lot. Like she enjoys it.

"Lockling Enterprises isn't just aviation. They hold stock in practically everything. Movie studios. Restaurant chains. Drive-ins. You name it; they have a finger in it. Virgil Thorne didn't want them gobbling up his company."

I feel sick. As if I've eaten a bowl of those expensive Russian fish eggs.

"I'm sorry." She winces. "My big mouth. She didn't tell you. A recent friend?"

"You could say that." I have to measure my words. "If you don't mind my asking, how do you know all this?"

Another quick laugh. "I read the newspapers. Not like it's top-secret."

"Huh."

She gives me a wink. "You should try it sometime."

"Try what?"

"Reading a newspaper." She starts to laugh again, then curbs it. "If you're going to be pals with Ania Thorne, you might want to get to know her crowd. Everyone knows everyone here. Or they think they do. They never forget a scandal. Or a new face."

"Neither do I."

"Good. Then we'll remember each other when we meet again. It was nice talking to you, Mr. New Face. Who knew? These parties are usually so boring." She starts to turn away in a swirl of skirts. Then stops. Casts a glance over her shoulder. "You never told me your name. Oh, well. Guess we need to give it time."

I watch her saunter off before turning back around. Ania walks toward me with an extra champagne flute. Around us, people start to drift into the ballroom, summoned by the orchestra. Sounds like a Cole Porter tune.

As I take the flute, I see her face. Cold. I know that look. Oh, boy, do I know it.

"What do you think you're doing?"

"Me?" I curb the urge to ask her about Mr. Impressive Jaw. "Why?"

"You were talking to her."

"Actually, she was talking to me."

"Jerome." She underscores my name. "A stranger. Have you lost your mind?"

"I told you. She was talking to me. Came right up to me, in fact. Friendly as California."

"Yes, well. She would be, wouldn't she?" Ania takes a moment. It's nerves. She might act as if diamond dust ices her veins, but I've felt the heat beneath it. The hidden core of lava. "Her mother is the socialite, Isabel Segal. Her father runs a movie studio. They approached us to lend them jewelry for a picture. We don't do that. The insurance risk is too high."

"She also reads newspapers. Seems to know a lot about you," I say.

"She doesn't." Ania lifts a hand to adjust her mask. "Finish your champagne. You're going to invite Marie Antoinette to dance, remember? It's showtime."

Chapter 2

Ania

The problem with Venice is the floods. Not the water, but the memories.

I sip my champagne. I'm allowing myself one glass for courage as I try to ignore the waves threatening to overwhelm me.

It doesn't help that I just ran into Hugh. I didn't expect him to be here. How foolish of me. So many of my firsts happened here. I should have known that Venice would also be the first place I'd commit a crime and stumble upon my ex-fiancé. It's just that the memories have become so much more difficult since discovering who my father is. Since he put me in harm's way. That's why I was reluctant to choose a particular Thorne piece to go after, and why I spent longer than I should have, trying to find another target. But no one's as careless as Julie, and no piece is more iconic than the Lemon Twist, as my father's masterpiece is known.

I cross the ballroom floor to stand by the windows overlooking the Grand Canal, the main venue of this mysterious, ancient city. As always, we're staying at my godmother's palazzo during this trip. The same palazzo my parents and I stayed in on our yearly visits for Carnival, and where I lived for my nineteenth year. My aunt is elderly and infirm now, residing in the south of France, but when I telephoned her to ask for permission to stay, she was delighted to turn over the keys. No one uses the palazzo anymore. Not since my mother—"

Watching a traghetto gondola pass on the churning waters, I find myself ruminating on those happier times. My mother taking me to get my mask and costume. Watching her be fitted for hers. My father clapping his hands when he saw us. He always used the same disguise— Shakespeare's *Merchant of Venice*. I even thought about having Jerome wear it tonight. It's still in the closet in the master bedroom where my parents stayed. But as soon as I thought of it, the idea of him taking my father's disguise seemed obscene. I still can't believe it occurred to me.

That's what Venice does. It floods. It unravels me.

I also have memories of the year I spent here on my own, designing a line of glass jewelry for one of my father's oldest friends. My first jewelry line. I stayed at the palazzo with my godmother, who was still very much on the circuit. It was at one of her Sunday soirees where I met Hugh—the first man I loved. Probably the last, if the anger and sadness that followed did what they were supposed to do.

It's all I can do not to turn around and look for him. But I'm not nineteen anymore. Hugh is, like so many things, in my past. It's been almost seven years. I'm a different woman now. With a new lover and reluctant accomplice.

It's not that Jerome can admit he has any qualms. He claims he wants revenge, too. Says he needs it. But as much as I do? Down deep in his bones? I don't think so. For him, it's a matter of pride. He wants to prove that he's up for it. I can appreciate that. I like a man who wants to show off a little. But he's in it for a taste. I'm in it for the feast. A hunger I've never experienced before, fueled by a fiery rage that won't be put out until I see my father brought to his knees—like he did to me in Cannes.

Taking another sip of my champagne, I turn around to survey the room, looking for Jerome without thinking I am. I thought I'd be nervous. Instead, all I feel is excitement. It astonishes me. All of my senses are on alert. My awareness of all the sights and sounds and scents is like an animal on the prowl.

I have about forty minutes before the dancing starts. My job now is to be seen chatting with friends. Catching up on the latest gossip and news. Make sure I look relaxed and as if I'm enjoying myself. And there's no reason not to. Julie might be as vulgar as a cheap markdown, but she knows how to throw a party. A live orchestra playing classic tunes. The finest champagne. The best canapes. When the servitor approaches, I make sure to take a caviar blini and a tiny ball of mozzarella marinated in basil oil.

If I were nervous, I wouldn't be able to take a bite.

My flute is nearly empty. Time for a refill. I make my way past a few revelers I know, stopping to say hello. There's the usual flirting behind the masks, the hope of indiscretion as if being in costume grants permission to throw morals aside, but that's too much for me to attempt tonight. I can mimic the gaiety. The night is young. Everyone knows they should be having fun, even if I can sense their ingrained reluctance, the social fear of *what-will-they-say?* They're all rich and guilty of sin, so no one should care. But they're still unsure of how to let go and indulge their base impulses. As the alcohol keeps flowing, that'll change. It will become less difficult.

I'm counting on it.

I glance at a gilded clock on the mantel, an exact replica of the famous clock in the Piazza San Marco done in gold, lapis lazuli, and ivory. One of Julie's acquisitions, no doubt. Tacky as her Hollywood movie posters. It's ten forty-five p.m. Fifteen minutes to go, and then I can leisurely make my way out of the public rooms and go upstairs.

Of course, that level isn't open to guests, but I won't look like one.

It wasn't difficult to uncover Julie's choice of attire. All I had to do was call her secretary, posing as a consultant for a high-profile guest, asking if the contessa had decided yet. Because my client wanted to make sure she didn't upstage Julie at her ball.

"Balenciaga," said her secretary coldly. "Couture. With her custom-made mantilla."

Which meant one-of-a-kind.

Like plucking a pearl from an open oyster. I own Balenciaga, too, so I just had to have a dress tailored in a similar style, in the same shade of black. A fringed Spanish wrap. Julie wasn't amused when she saw me upon our arrival.

"Oh, my," she said, her pinched smile not touching her eyes. "What a coincidence. Cristobal is such a liar. He assured me that mine was the only one."

"It is. Mine is Dior," I purred, kissing her cheeks. Too much No. 5. She must have bathed in it. It couldn't disguise her fury that we're dressed alike.

Anyone glimpsing me tonight as I take the stairs won't pay attention to the hostess heading up to her rooms. If they happen to then see her on the dance floor—well, the champagne is flowing, as I said. Who can say what they saw first?

The magic hour approaches. I need to prepare.

"Ania."

I turn.

Ah, Venice. You can stop it with the floods. When Hugh and I greeted each other briefly, I assumed that would be the worst. I don't want to re-visit the past or make chitchat and was sure he didn't either, especially after his date inserted herself into our greeting. She practically shoved me aside in her resolve to stake her claim. I don't play those games. I said goodnight and retreated. I'd assumed that was it. Now, I wonder if some conversations never really end.

"I'm sorry for the interruption," Hugh says, his date discarded somewhere in the crowd with him standing so close I can smell his familiar scent of rosemary and mint, along with a hint of the cherry-pipe tobacco he favors. A pipe, not cigarettes. Harvard men only smoke pipes.

I can't help myself. I still feel something. It's not only that you don't forget your first love. It's that your first love changes who you are. Alters you. And if that first love ends badly, then the *what-ifs* lodge in your heart and your life. Here's the man who made me vow never to give away that part of my heart again. And he's smiling the same smile I remember, taking me by the elbow in the same way he always did, leaning to my ear to whisper, "Let's dance. Before she finds me."

"Really?" I let out a brittle laugh, tilting my head back just enough to let him know. "Maybe you should dance with her first. Then we'll see about later."

He falters just for a second. Hugh never lets himself be too taken aback.

"You look gorgeous, Ania. I can't believe it. You haven't changed a bit."

"Oh, I have."

"What?" He doesn't take his smoky-grey eyes from mine. "The schlub in the white tie, looking like he's missing a tray of canapes to serve? That's my competition?"

"Hugh." I prop a hand on my cocked hip. "Please don't start."

"I was just asking." He grins. Those perfect white teeth. "Guy ought to know who he needs to tackle on the field."

I thought I'd never get over this man, not even after discovering that my father was right about him. Hugh wanted Thorne & Company for the Lockling crown as much as he wanted me. Maybe more. When I confronted him about it, demanding the truth, he insisted that it wasn't a betrayal. Yes, his father hoped to acquire the company, but he'd eventually inherit Lockling Enterprises, and then it would all be ours. And he did everything to try and prove it, proposing to me on my twentieth birthday. He asked for my hand here, in Venice. Not during a cliché gondola ride—that would have been too rote. After a lavish dinner at Harry's, we walked over to the Palazzo Ducale and the San Giorgio Maggiore church. He led me into the nave, past a path lit by tapers, to a staircase. As we climbed, he kept his hand on the small of my back for the entire one hundred steps. Upon reaching the campanile, the bell tower had a table, a bottle of champagne in a silver bucket, and two of my favorite ruby Murano glass flutes atop it. Hugh and I stood at the railing, looking out over the city, viewing what seemed like the entire world. Like two conquerors.

"Marry me," he said. Not going to one knee but proffering a velvet box the same color as the midnight sky. Inside? An exquisite emerald-cut diamond—which I knew immediately was from the Golconda mines and was at least a century old. Only Golconda diamonds have that liquidity. Like pure water frozen in time. I also knew because I was well-aware of that particular ring. Every jeweler and collector is. The Lockling diamond had been his grandmother's, acquired from an auction of the Romanov treasures in 1925.

Not a Thorne stone or setting, which pleased me more than expected. At the time, I wasn't sure why.

I said yes, of course. After a passionate kiss, Hugh popped the cork, and we toasted each other. The Venetian lights. The Italian night. The world of possibilities to conquer.

I wore the ring for three months. Until my father—

No, I won't think about that now.

"As I was saying before we were so rudely interrupted—" he starts.

"By your date."

"By someone I brought to the party. As I was saying, I didn't know you'd be here."

"I didn't know you studied the guest list of the parties you attend."

"Actually, I do. I'm always looking for you."

I sigh. I expect it can't be true. But Hugh has a way of saying the most over-the-top nonsense and making it sound sincere. Like how he used to call me *darling*. I wouldn't have let anyone else call me that, not even my father. But there was an insouciance to the way he said it that somehow made it work.

"Let's not do this," I say. "How are you? How are the twins?"

I regret my question at once. It betrays that I've kept tabs on him, too. I actually haven't. I just happened to read in the society pages about his wedding four years ago to a socialite, a former girlfriend from his Harvard days, and then the twins born a few weeks early. *Quelle surprise.*

"The twins are fine. With their mom in Palm Beach. We're getting a divorce."

"I'm sorry to hear it." I assumed as much. "That explains the date."

He nods. "You know, darling, I wouldn't be divorced at all if…"

He plucks my hand, turning it over to kiss my palm. I pull away as if it burns. This is no time to rekindle old flames. And yet, I can't help but think my father is no longer the head of Thorne & Company. Merging it with Lockling Enterprises would go far in more than one way at getting back at him. He'd be so enraged.

"What's wrong? I'm single again. You're single—you still are, aren't you? You can't tell me it's anything serious with the schlub."

I glance over my shoulder, suddenly needing to see Jerome. He's talking with some redhead in a garish green dress. Is that…? God. Lauren Segal. On the hunt. Not getting any younger, and despite her Hollywood fortune, no viable prospects on the horizon. I feel a frisson of a different sort. Not nostalgic or bittersweet.

Raw. Territorial. An animal instinct to claw.

"You really should give me another chance," Hugh says. "You're running the company now. Your father can't interfere."

"Honestly, Hugh. Don't you think this is a little fast? Not to mention, years too late? We bump into each other here, and suddenly, you're declaring yourself?"

"I've just been thinking about you a lot since…I heard what happened at the Carlton. We were there for the film festival. I reached out to you but never heard back."

"You did?" I'm taken aback; though, like him, I never let myself be.

"Yes. Of course, I did. The concierge told me you'd left the hotel. I didn't know where you were. I even tried to call your father to find out."

"He never said."

"Well, he wouldn't, would he?"

I nod. It's much too complicated to discuss my father with him, of all people.

"Anyway, I tried. Can I see you while we're in Venice? For dinner, at least? Or lunch, if that's better? There are things we should discuss."

Do I want to? Does what I want matter anymore? I'm here on a mission, and he's not part of it. Except perhaps he might come in handy if I ever need help at some point. Not that I will, but better to keep my options open.

"I'm staying at the palazzo," I hear myself say.

"How is your aunt?"

"She's old. Frail. She's almost ninety now."

"Yes. I'm sorry."

"It happens. Hugh, I'm not sure if we should—"

Before I can finish, his pushy brunette date dressed as a butterfly sidles up to us and interrupts again. My, but she's a determined little thing, isn't she? Not stupid, either. All that Lockling cash on the line.

"You promised me a dance, Hughie." She actually pouts.

Hughie?

She probably thinks it's sexy. I smile and extricate myself.

I have work to do.

"I'm at the Danieli," he calls out after me.

After returning to Jerome to chide him for talking to Lauren—whatever is he thinking, she's a stranger—and sending him into the ballroom to find Julie, I fetch my wrap from the coat check and head to the foyer. The main staircase is to the right. To the left, the back quarters of the palazzo—the servant area. I slip my wrap around my shoulders and make my way up the stairs as if I own the place.

Which is the idea.

Anyone walking through the foyer will see Julie from the back, my dress and wrap nearly identical to hers.

Julie, gone to deposit her vintage Thorne so she doesn't lose it while dancing.

Chapter 3

Ania

I'm about to try a door when I hear someone coming up the stairs. I melt into the shadows, watching. A man pauses at the landing, looking down into the foyer, using the vantage point to survey the area as if trying to catch something he thought was there. He isn't wearing a mask. No costume or tuxedo, either. Just a large man with broad shoulders in a bland, dark suit. He doesn't look like a guest to me. I've never seen him before. I back up as carefully as I can, reaching for the doorknob behind me, turning it and praying it doesn't squeak as I slip inside.

That was too close.

I concentrate on the room before me to slow my heart, which is pounding. How did my father do this? How long did it take him to learn to keep control at all times during his heists? But he didn't, did he? He killed a young woman when she came upon him, rifling through a vault in London. Murdered her in cold blood. A mistake. He made them.

I can't afford to make one now.

The room I entered is done up in forest green and gold. Lots of gold. From the tassels on the heavy velvet drapes to the foot of the molding that frames the wall. I note a man's suit on the silent butler, male accessories on the dresser.

A bedroom. Maybe the absent count's? Not the one I'm looking for.

How long should I wait? Who was that man on the stairs? Is it safe for me to venture back into the corridor? Probably not. In my godmother's palazzo, a terrace runs along the upper floor that allows access from one room to the next—if the doors aren't locked from the inside. The floorplan Jerome found at the Accademia showed the same layout here. Most of Venice's palazzos have identical floorplans, all built during the Renaissance. Surely, it's safer to try the terrace route than risk going out into the corridor again.

I open the inside doors and step onto the terrace, feeling the sharp sting of the cold as I move left in the direction of what I believe must be the other main bedroom. I went over the palazzo's layout and the plan what seemed a thousand times with Jerome. He insisted on it. We only counted five doors. Not six.

Did he have the right floorplan?

It's damp and dripping outside. Typical Venetian winter. A mist hovers over the canal. That's good; it'll hide me if anyone happens to look up. They'll think they saw a ghost. In a city full of them, what's one more?

I reach the next room and peer inside. Yes. The one I'm searching for. I hold my breath as I try the terrace door's handle. It turns. I have to smile. A woman who leaves her jewels out in the open never thinks about locking her doors. It's a miracle nobody has burglarized her already.

I step inside, recognizing the blue-and-gold master bedroom from photographs I've seen in magazines of Julie posing in her Venetian palazzo: the movie star at home. It's also a mess. Couture strewn about without any regard for its value. Hats and gloves and shoes dropped like damaged goods. By the bed, a Murano glass bowl. I recognize the style of my favorite glassblowing factory located on the lagoon on the island of Murano. The firm I used to work for. A company owned by my father's friend. I created necklaces and earrings for them, rings and bracelets in the most vivid colors. Emeralds, rubies, citrines, diamonds: all made of glass and blown by the artists. Quite expensive for glass. They sold well and still do. I should include some in a new collection.

If I ever design again.

More valuable pieces rest in the bowl. Gold chains twisted through Verdura Maltese cross bangles. The kind Coco Chanel wore. My father always said Verdura had lucked out—meaning he was all charm and good taste, not a great designer. He had the luck, Papa said, to hire artists who knew what they were doing. And luck that Chanel took a liking to his pieces. Having her photographed in his matching onyx and gold cuffs made them instant classics.

But I don't want the Verdura. I want the Thorne. And just as I suspected, I find the Lemon Twist on the vanity table alongside another Murano glass dish full of a half-dozen rings in a riot of colors. It pains me to see all these precious pieces tossed together as if they're cheap costume jewelry.

Julie never had any class.

I pick up the diamond necklace. One of my father's most famous. Made right after the war, with a stone that legend says saved a village in Russia during the pogroms. Apparently, a Jewish diamond dealer owned the round, twenty-one-carat canary diamond at the center and traded it for enough to help him, his entire family, and most of the small village escape to New York. The diamond was then sold to a sugar heiress who had Cartier mount it in a brooch. Her children split up her inheritance and put the diamond up for auction at Sotheby's. That was when my father acquired it. He set it in reverse with its facets showing alongside graduated white and canary rounds, forming a shimmering circlet, everything set backwards to attract the light.

It was unheard of at the time—a setting as revolutionary as the events that brought the stone to America. A diamond is cut for its table, but he'd noticed that the canary had such an unusual facet pattern from the back, it made it more alluring.

Now, I have it. I have to get out of the room and return to Jerome. Accomplish the next step. It's still hard for me to have a partner. He's dancing with the contessa, creating our alibi. If I would only admit it, the truth is, it soothes me knowing he's downstairs. I think of Hugh in the same room. Both of them circling each other on the dance floor.

I wonder, not for the first time, why Jerome ever agreed to this. He devoted his life to doing the right thing. I've tempted him into something wrong. I should feel guilty, but I don't. At least, not yet. Maybe I will once the thrill wears off. When I get used to his presence. When I become accustomed to the incredible intensity of how well we fit in bed. When I get tired of what he calls "slumming it."

"Why would I?" I once asked him.

"Because girls like you always do," he joked. "Don't you watch movies?"

"I prefer to live my own adventures than see one on the screen," I replied.

And here I am, living my adventure. Not exactly what I had in mind, though.

I slip the diamond necklace into my wristlet, move back out onto the terrace and along the narrow parapet through the mist, and into the neighboring guest suite.

The trip back downstairs is uneventful. Whoever the man was, he's nowhere to be seen. I remove my wrap, return it and my wristlet to the cloakroom, then enter the ballroom. Jerome is still dancing. He looks miserable, even if I had the hardest job of the night. Mingling with the crowd, pretending to be enjoying myself...

Hugh materializes with two flutes of champagne. He offers me one.

"What should we toast?" he says. "To fortuitous meetings in foreign cities?"

I nod, and we clink glasses. Just like old times. Except nothing is like old times.

Back then, I wasn't a thief.

"Let's dance," I say. "For old times' sake."

Might as well enjoy myself a little.

Chapter 4

Jerome

I'm swell at plenty of things. Dancing isn't one of them. I can make my way through a basic foxtrot because, growing up, it was part of what schools in my day called "deportment for boys." But, really, I'm faking it. I like jazz, the unpredictable riff and trill of it. You can't follow any choreography to it. You have to feel it. In your soul.

But the contessa doesn't seem to notice that I've stepped on her toes one too many times. She clings to me like a clam to a shell, her hot breath a mix of alcohol and movie-star seduction. Her eyes are bloodshot, her blue-spangled mask askew so its peacock plume keeps brushing my chin. She's drunk. Or on her way to it. But whenever the music calls for a closer encounter, she's right on it, her voluptuous body in her black dress cleaving to every inch of mine. Her hips in particular. Despite her oversaturation of champagne, she seems to know exactly where my groin is located.

She must be disappointed. My groin certainly is.

I restrain myself from looking over her shoulder, past the other couples crowding the floor, to the far entrance of her grandiose ballroom where Ania should appear at any minute. It's hot as hell in here. All these people in clothing that weighs a ton, all the candles guttering, the aroma of overcooked food on burners in the buffet room, thick as grease. I'm starting to feel sick. I really want a cigarette. And fresh air. If you can ever find that in a city half-submerged under seawater that stinks like sushi.

Where is Ania? As the orchestra launches into a swing tune from a time I don't recall as being fun at all, the dancefloor erupts, headdresses swaying and threatening to impale bystanders, fistfuls of those flammable skirts bunched up as the high-society club prances and gyrates like Santa's reindeer.

Whenever I hear swing, all I see are bodies. Skeletal limbs. Piled like kindling by imploded crematoria. Refuse left behind by monsters fleeing to Berlin.

I must make an indication of discomfort or falter somehow because the contessa's arms snake around my sweaty neck—my white tie likely not looking so white now—as she says, "Don't worry. She's here. Somewhere. Anyway, she's never been one to care."

"Care?" I shouldn't ask. It's probably not a good idea to talk shop with the target.

"You know." She pushes her face toward mine, her mouth open. Revulsion curdles in me. "Jealousy is so bourgeois. And, well—" Christ, is she going to kiss me right here in the middle of her ballroom? "It's not her style. I'm sure she thinks it's very shocking, bringing the help as her date, but that too-rich-for-his-own-good aviation heir is much more her type. While you... Oh, you're mine. So rough. I bet you're very rough. Aren't you?"

I'm about to push her away, excuse myself with the uncontrollable urge to vomit, when I suddenly spot Ania. She glides into the room as if she went to powder her nose, her slim column of black silk molding to her ballerina legs. She pauses, gazing upon the pandemonium with what I know is a wry look under her perfectly placed mask.

Relief floods me. I can't rush over to her. Even if I could, the contessa has me in a vise. As I narrowly avoid crushing her toes again, I see Lauren Segal, dancing and laughing with an overweight guy in a monocle and a Napoleonic hat. Boring party or not, she's definitely having fun. She catches my eye and gives me a wink.

It's just what I need to relax. Ania must have done it. Without a hitch.

Until the contessa lugs me around again, the orchestra starting up another slow Porter tune. As her hips meld right back to where I don't want them, I catch sight of Ania again, setting her glass aside to move onto the floor, hand in hand with Mr. Impressive Jaw.

They could almost be mistaken for brother and sister. Almost. But the way his palm comes to rest right where her skin shows under the scoop of her dress, the way he cocks his head and regards her with his smoky eyes as they sway to *You Do Something to Me*, it's not brotherly at all.

The guy is making his move on her.

I see red. I want to punch him right in his impressive jaw.

Ania doesn't look at me, though I'm a short distance away, getting mauled by the drunken ex-starlet whose necklace we just stole. When she shifts her shoulders like a cat at the end of the tune, and the too-rich aviation heir suddenly bends to kiss Ania's neck, I wait to see her flinch. Maybe slap him across his face.

Instead, she slips out of his arms and retreats to her discarded glass. I can read the way she moves. Not a dismissal. But close. He stands alone for a moment, bemused as the orchestra takes a break, and the dancers stampede to the overcooked food at the buffet, shedding sequins and bits of feathers.

"Well." The contessa releases me and drops her bloodshot eyes to my disinterested crotch. "I guess she's more your type than you are hers. A shame."

It's eerie to see how fast she switches from come-hither to you-can't-touch-me. Maybe she isn't as drunk as I thought. She walks away as though she hasn't just tried to lure me into her marriage bed, her head high, smiling as her fawning guests emerge from the buffet with overflowing plates of shellfish, garnished veal, and miniature fruit pyramids.

When I see her straighten her mask, putting herself to rights, then move with sure-footed determination to the entry leading to the staircase, my stomach drops to my feet.

I don't run. I walk as quickly as I can to Ania, who's holding her glass like an accessory. Before I can utter a word, she says, "I have it."

"I think you might want to re-think that."

"Get a glass of champagne."

"What?"

"Get. A glass. Of champagne. Now."

I lurch to a nearby side table and search the mess of half-filled glasses for one that doesn't have lipstick smudges. When I return to her, she says, "We stick to the plan. We don't leave until others do. We were here all night. Everyone saw us."

"She's going upstairs, Ania."

"And?" She raises her glass to sip. So calm. *How* can she be so calm?

"And? And she's going to see her necklace isn't there!"

"It doesn't matter."

"You bet, it matters. When she sees it's gone, it'll matter a whole—"

A scream so loud it freezes everyone in the ballroom rents the air, bringing guests staggering from the buffet, forks halfway to their mouths. I start to take Ania's arm, a primal impulse to shield her overtaking me. She steps back and fixes me with a hard glare.

And then Julie Kimbell's frantic wail sounds, the one heard by moviegoers across America as her on-screen gladiator lover battled ravenous lions in the Colosseum.

"My necklace! *Someone has stolen my fucking necklace!*"

Moments later, she lunges back into the ballroom, followed by a guy as big as a boulder. I can't believe it. A bodyguard. Here. All night. I didn't see him. Where was he?

"Who did it?" Julie waves her hands. "*Who* has it?"

She's clutching something. A piece of cloth. What is that...?

And then it hits me. Like I imagine her bodyguard's fist would feel in my gut.

A leopard-print glove.

I can't move. I can't breathe.

"Motherfuckers," I hear Julie gasp. "No one leaves. I'm calling the *polizia.*" She whirls to her boulder bodyguard. "Get them on the phone this instant. Tell them I've been robbed."

Boulder takes a moment to assess her frozen audience. Not a sound. Not a movement. Like everyone, every person on her exclusive guest list has been reduced to voiceless paralysis.

Until Mr. Impressive Jaw steps forth to murmur, "Julie. Please. Calm down."

"*Calm down?*" She lets out an ear-piercing shriek. Those acting lessons sure are coming in handy now. "Someone stole my—"

He reaches out and takes her by the arm. "Not someone here, Julie. That glove."

She looks at her hand, then drops the glove as if it's contagious. "Oh. God. No." And just like that, Julie Kimbell, nee Anna-May Kimsky, star of B-movies and Contessa of Maglione, collapses into the aviation heir's embrace. Sobbing and helpless.

Boulder turns to march into the foyer, carving an inexorable path through the hired staff standing motionless with party detritus piled on platters.

As Hugh Lockling guides the distraught victim to a chair, the room surges into gasps of dismay and a consoling mob around her.

I turn my eyes to Ania.

She's not smiling. But I see it anyway. The smile within.

The Leopard left his signature mark on Julie's nightstand.

And just as I thought, we're in a heap of trouble.

Within a half-hour, the Italian police are swarming the palazzo, arriving crammed into siren-wailing motorboats like something out of a Marx Brothers movie, clambering up the landing steps to sequester us in the ballroom as they undertake the search.

Then a portly man waddles into the ballroom. Receded hairline and annoyed expression, his suit rumpled and tie undone, a spaghetti stain on his shirt cuff, indicating that he was likely interrupted at his late-night pasta dinner. He ignores the guests gathered in herds like frightened prey, though not so frightened they didn't manage to finish off the rest of the buffet while Julie wept disconsolately.

Hugh Lockling has stayed stalwart at her side, offering glasses of water she waves away and murmuring reassurances. The latter, I notice, she hasn't waved away. She doesn't look as if she believes whatever he's telling her, but having his masculine attention focused solely on her in her moment of crisis is obviously welcome.

The portly man motions Lockling aside like he's an unwanted glass of water and proceeds to question Julie in rapid-fire Italian.

Ania and I haven't moved from our place near the side table with its discarded champagne glasses, even as staff members gingerly remove most of it and disappear into what I assume is the kitchen. After pocketing the glove that Julie dropped, Boulder directs them to pick up where they halted now that the police are here. They tiptoe like ghosts about the guests, tidying up as if their lives depend on it.

I snort. "What? The help isn't considered suspects?" As I say this, I recall what Julie called me on the dancefloor.

"Hush." Ania has her arms folded across her chest as if it's all a minor inconvenience that we must endure. But her focus, like her ex-fiancé's, is on Julie.

"What's he saying?" I can barely order a coffee in Italian, much less decipher his volley. Ania is fluent. One of the perks of being a rich girl who vacationed in Italy every year.

"The usual. Where was she when the necklace went missing? When did she last see it? Why did she leave it upstairs? Etcetera."

It strikes me that I used to do his job. Drill past the etcetera to the gist of the crime. He must be the investigator. The chief inspector, or *sostituto commissario,* as they're called here. My Italian is abysmal, but I know this much because I made certain to check it out, in order to determine the risk. It had seemed negligible. Following Mussolini's crackdown on Venetian frolic and Italy's collaboration with the Germans during the war, the police here aren't what you'd describe as well-funded. They manage to keep crime at bay, but Venice is a small, internecine city populated by impoverished old families and ex-pats. Anything more violent than a random pickpocketing of a neglectful tourist is rare.

But then he straightens and turns around. Starts waddling toward us.

"Uh-oh," I mutter under my breath.

"Just keep calm," Ania says. "I know him. It's fine."

She removes her mask as he approaches. He has a large beak of a nose and close-set, metallic-dark eyes.

"Ah, Signorina Thorne. Such a pleasure to see you in Venezia again." His wispy voice startles me, coming from such a heavyset man.

His English is accented, much better than my Italian. Melodious with a hint of old-fashioned fascism. I half expect him to click his heels and bow over her hand.

Ania smiles. "*Commissario* Gabrielli. Lovely to see you, as well. If not under these circumstances."

"*Sì.* A pity, yes? *La pobre* contessa..." He extracts a handkerchief from his jacket and swabs his brow. He's sweating. Guess it's too hot in here for him, too. For some reason, the ordinary gesture isn't comforting. I have the sense he's not as befuddled as he looks.

"Yes. Poor Julie. Can we be of any help?" prompts Ania.

"No. I don't think so. Actually..." With his handkerchief still in his hand, he rubs pensively at his chin. A theatrical pause. "*La contessa* tells me she was dancing with your American friend before the incident, yes? Is this him?"

Ania nods. "Yes, this is him."

"Does the *Americano* have a name?"

"Jerome." I extend my hand. "Jerome Curtis."

He shakes my hand briefly. His palm is moist. "*Parli Italiano?*"

"I'm sorry—"

"No problem. We speak English, yes?"

His habit of ending every sentence with a question makes it hard to figure out if he's being rhetorical. "Yeah. Sure," I say.

"So. You were dancing all night with the contessa?"

"Not all night." I hear my quick denial and make myself slow down. "We were having drinks before. In the foyer. With the other guests."

"With the contessa?"

"With me," says Ania. "Julie was there, naturally. It's her party. She likes to greet all the guests as they arrive. But we weren't having drinks with her at the time."

"But later, yes? In the ballroom?" The inspector gives me a knowing smile, a man of the world. A former movie star, married to an absent count. Drinks before dancing. It's to be expected.

I pretend to search my mind. "No," I say.

"No?" His unkempt eyebrows lift.

"No. I didn't have drinks with her in the ballroom. She was talking with one of her guests, and I asked her if she wanted to dance."

"How gallant." Again, the old-fashioned manners. "And she said yes?"

"Yes. I mean, she said yes. She wanted to dance."

"I see." A moment of silence. "And afterward?"

"After we danced? She went upstairs. I came over here to be with Ania."

"Ah. Yes. *La bella* Signorina Thorne." He smiles at her. Paternal, as if he can remember seeing her in pigtails, skipping across the Piazza San Marco.

"And then?"

"Then?" I echo.

"Yes. Then what happened?"

"Nothing happened."

"Nothing?" The unkempt eyebrows go up again.

"We were having a glass of champagne," Ania says. "We heard Julie scream. She came rushing downstairs. Very upset."

"Ah." A grimace of commiseration. "How can she not be? Such a valuable necklace."

"My father designed it." Ania smiles. "I know it well."

"Ah. *La contessa* mentioned this. Your company wanted it back for—how do you say? —historic purposes. She refused, yes?"

"We did. She did." Ania lets out a sigh. "Such is business. We took no offense. It's her property, after all. She wasn't obliged."

"I see."

Does he? I think he does—a lot more than we'd like.

"Well." He dabs once again at his forehead. "All these other people." He sounds resigned. A long night of work. His pasta dinner getting cold.

"Are we free to go?" asks Ania.

"Oh." He pauses as if it hadn't occurred to him. "Yes. I think so. You're staying in Venezia for Carnival?"

Ania nods. "At my aunt's palazzo."

"And Signor Thorne?"

"He didn't come. The memories…he can't anymore."

"Ah. Yes. The memories. Such a lovely woman, Signora Thorne. She is missed."

"She is." A catch in Ania's voice.

"*Prego.* You may go. It is late. But." He inclines his head in regret. "Please don't leave the city without informing us, yes? This incident…we must do our duty."

"Of course. I understand. You know where to find us should you need anything."

"Yes. *Grazie*, signorina. Always a pleasure." He moves off toward the herd.

I stare after him until I feel Ania's hand on my arm. "Come on. It's over."

But as she fetches her wrap and wrist-bag from the coat check and we depart the palazzo under the nod of a policeman standing guard, then board her gondola with the chill of winter glazing the air and my sweat-soaked white tie, I think it's far from over.

From what I can tell, it's just started.

Chapter 5

Jerome

She doesn't say anything on the ride back. Just as well. I'm freezing now in the clammy mist shrouding the city—it's very scenic, all these ancient, floating buildings, but a permanent case of athlete's foot to live in. When we arrive, I leap from the gondola onto the palazzo quay, eager to get inside and out of these clothes. Then I remember and turn to offer her my hand. She rolls her eyes and gets out of the gondola by herself.

The staff has retired, leaving lights on for us in the foyer. She goes straight into the living area, draping her wrap on the uncomfortable damask sofa, then moves to the bar cart. She doesn't switch on any lamps, but I hear the clink of a glass, the bottle being poured.

It's the only sign the night has taken its toll. She never drinks much. Neither do I. I stand hesitant, watching her silhouette limned by the gothic window overlooking the canal. Not much of a view now, just dense fog and the distant pinprick of lamps.

"I'm going to take a quick shower," I say, for lack of anything better.

"Okay." Her voice is muted.

I head upstairs. In the shower, I bask under the tepid stream of water. Like the rest of Venice, water pressure and heating are behind the times. After drying off and slipping into my old jeans and sweater, I rake a hand through my damp hair and feel how short it is. She insisted on a barber before the ball. The hair reminds me of Mr. Impressive Jaw's immaculate crewcut. I scowl and return to the living room.

She's still at the window, nursing her glass.

"What are you drinking?" I ask.

"Whiskey."

"Wow." I serve myself some, though I've had enough champagne to guarantee an ugly hangover.

I don't know what to do. What to say. I stand by the cart, observing her profile etched against the night, and all I can think is how beautiful she looks. How lonely.

I'm sure she thinks it's very shocking, bringing the help as her date...

"We didn't think this through well." It comes busting out.

"No?" She half turns to me. I can't see her expression. Too much shadow.

"No. Mr. Pasta seems to have taken an unhealthy interest in your *Americano*."

A dry laugh. "Gabrielli is an old family friend. He and my father—" A terse pause. The hesitation. Always now, whenever he comes up. "They used to meet at Harry's and play chess. He's known me since I was a girl. Of course, he took an interest in you."

"I don't mean it that way."

"Then in what way did you mean?" She walks past me to the cart and sets down her glass. She's barely touched it. She moves to the sofa, to her wrap and wrist-bag.

When I don't speak, she does. "Jerome. Please, just say it. I'm too tired for this."

I gulp my whiskey, feeling it burn my mouth and throat. "Why didn't you tell me?"

"Tell you what?"

"The glove. We never planned that. You never told me—"

She cuts me off. "I thought it was assumed."

"Assumed?"

A trace of impatience. "We needed the heist to look like he did it, right?"

"We took one of his favorite pieces." I can't control the sudden anger in my voice. "During a gala where, according to Lauren Segal, no one forgets a scandal. Or a new face."

"Is that what's bothering you? Lauren Segal?"

I take a step toward her. "What's bothering me is that you went ahead and did something without telling me. You placed a glove at the scene. You put us at risk for—"

"For what?" She meets my stare.

"I don't know. You tell me."

Her answer is to reach for her wrist-bag, yank it open, and dump the necklace onto her wrap on the sofa. It doesn't look so valuable now. Smaller somehow. Cheaper, like Lauren Segal's muddy emeralds.

"You...you put it in your *bag*?"

"Where did you want me to put it? I'm not wearing underwear under this dress."

"Neither was Marie Antoinette." My sudden laughter is harsh, like acid. "Jesus, Ania. The police were crawling all over the joint. They could have searched the coat check. Hell, they *should* have searched it. What in God's name were you thinking?"

"According to you, I wasn't. Thinking, that is."

"Look." I try to soften my tone, reduce the tension. We're both on edge. We have stolen property on the sofa. "It wasn't part of our plan."

"So you keep saying."

"Ania. It wasn't. The glove. The police. You stashed the loot in your bag in plain sight. I bet it'll be in all the newspapers. She's an actress. She caused a scene. A hundred and twenty people saw all of it go down."

"Not all of it. They saw what I wanted them to see. And, yes, it'll be in the newspapers. Julie will probably host a luncheon for reporters. That's how it's supposed to go. We agreed. To lure him out, we must bait the trap. This is how we do it."

I feel myself gaping at her, a lump in my throat. "I thought we were a team."

"We are. I didn't force you to do this, did I?"

"Goddammit." I bang my glass down with enough force to clang it on the table. "My ass could end up in the sling. You think your old family friend is going to let up because he used to play chess with your father? He just told us not to leave the city without informing him. What if he decides to confiscate the passports of everyone at the ball? What then?"

"He won't. It's Italy. Every person at that ball spends a lot of money in this city. They rent palazzos. Go to restaurants. Buy couture. Gabrielli is Venetian. He won't. He can't."

"Really? After a very valuable necklace was just stolen from a former movie star married to a rich Italian count, who also happens to be Venetian? You're nuts. This incident... We have to do our duty. What do you think his duty is? Wait for someone to come forth and confess? Hey, it was my mistake, Signor Inspector. Here it is. No problem."

She regards me without emotion. Like her mask is still on. "Now, who's causing a scene?"

I suddenly want to shake her. It's so unexpected and so searing, I have to move back.

"I was here," I tell her. "In Italy. After the war. I know how it works. They deported Jews. They let the Germans dictate it. They killed their own people. They don't give a shit about palazzos or couture. They care about not looking like shits after what they did."

She looks down. Just one glance at the necklace. "I did what had to be done," she says quietly. "If I'd told you, you would have tried to talk me out of it."

"Yes. I would have. Because it wasn't necessary."

"It was." Her face rears up. Oh, she's angry now. Finally, some heat to stoke her lava. "How do you think this makes me feel? How? Have you stopped to consider it? I should be in Los Angeles. In New York. Paris. Managing my company. Designing my jewelry. Not skulking about Julie's palazzo, stealing a necklace my father designed that she refused to exchange because—because he—" She falters. "None of this was my plan. None of it."

I absorb her words in silence, listening to the slight catch in her breathing. The fury she hides deep inside. Like she hides everything she finds threatening.

"Does none of it include me?" I finally ask.

"What is that supposed to mean?"

"C'mon. The aviation guy. Too rich for his own good. The kiss on the neck to Cole Porter. Good times. Your ex-fiancé."

She stares at me. I see the ice surface in her eyes. It hurts me like nothing else. "Are you serious? You're accusing me of…what?"

"I'm not accusing you of anything. I asked a question. Does none of it include me? Would you rather be back in Los Angeles or New York or Paris without me?"

"Right now? Yes." She turns about, moving toward the staircase. She pauses at the threshold. Doesn't look at me. "Hugh Lockling is a part of my past. I have one. Everyone does. He's not part of this. If you want to make him a part of it, go ahead. But I'm tired. I want to take a hot bath and get some sleep. Alone."

I listen to her climb the stairs. The fading echo of her heels. The groan of the old pipes as she turns on the faucet in the master bathroom. The door shutting.

The silence is heavy. Oppressive. I feel like I can't breathe. I know I should go up to her and apologize. Or just let her be for tonight. To soak in the tub, get a good night's rest, and pretend that nothing happened in the morning. That's her style. Brush it under the carpet, the unpleasantness. That's what rich people do. They don't re-hash sins.

I can't bear it. I grab my whiskey, down it, and then go up to the guest room, rummaging in my suitcase for my boots, my battered field coat, and a wool cap. I didn't pack enough, as usual. I didn't stop to think that Venice in January would be as inhospitable as Berlin.

How do you think this makes me feel? How? Have you stopped to consider it?

Throwing on my coat and cap and taking up my Lucky Strikes, I grab the extra key from the hook near the door and leave the palazzo by the side entrance that gives way to a narrow lane. One of the hundreds of labyrinthine streets winding about the city like coils, designed to get you totally lost. Wandering for hours, bumping into dead ends or stumbling onto murky canals without any bridge to cross.

Fine. I'll get lost. I light a cigarette. Relish the acrid inhale into my lungs.

I'll get lost so I don't have to think about how she'd rather be without me.

Chapter 6

Ania

I fill the bath with the special *Vidal Profumi* scented oils in the glass beakers and bottles around the tub. In the morning, my favorite is their eucalyptus gel. At night, I always chose the Bulgari Rose oil with a hint of lavender. It was my mother's favorite. I think about her for a few moments as I sink into the fragrant water.

Mama was always insatiably curious. One year, she decided she wanted to learn more about perfume in Venice, so we studied its history, surprised to learn that this was the center of European perfumery in the thirteenth century due to Venice being the trading crossroads for spices and incenses imported from the Far East. She was so enthused, she had us take a perfume-making class. She laughed when we made Papa smell our test scents and he gagged, declaring the plague would have never struck Venice had we been in charge. Our perfume would have killed the rats.

I sink deeper into the warm water, letting it wash over me.

Did Mama always try to learn new things because she felt she had less to give? Not the towering talent in the family, the genius. Were her attempts to draw me into her quests her way of ensuring that I would carry a part of her, too, not just as my father's daughter?

I can't ask her now. All the questions I have. No one to ask.

My body thrums. Is this how my father felt afterwards? This heady combination of accomplishment and awe? A disturbing sensation bubbles up in me as I think about him learning about the heist. What he'll think when he learns that he, the Leopard, has struck again, though he didn't actually do it; and stealing one of his most valuable and well-known early pieces—one that he'd tried in vain several times to have returned to us? How long will it take before he realizes that I'm responsible for the theft? And what will his reaction be? I wish I could see his face. His fury. And maybe his terse, unwitting smile of pride. His daughter in every way.

Even in ways he had never expected.

But we're not home-free yet.

My ass could end up in the sling. You think your family friend is going to let up because he used to play chess with your father?

Now, I have my temperamental partner-in-crime to deal with. I shouldn't have said what I did. It wasn't fair. That's the thing with Jerome. He manages to push buttons in me that no one has before. Buttons he shouldn't know exist. I've made sure all my life, especially after Hugh, to never let any man near those buttons. I'm the one who decides when to call the shots. I say when it starts and when it ends. But Jerome…he knows his way past my defenses. He knows just what to say to collapse them.

He was right. I should have told him about the glove. Why didn't I?

Wrapping myself in one of the plush, salmon-colored towels, I get out of the bath and put on the white robe draped on the towel warmer. It's as comforting as a hug. Safer, too. I don't have to explain myself to a robe. Don't have to justify why I was talking to Hugh. Or why I left the glove at the scene without informing Jerome of my plan.

My choice. My fall to take if it comes to that.

Except, it's not.

It's late. And I'm so tired all of a sudden. The adrenaline draining away, leaving exhaustion in its place. I leave the bedroom and go downstairs, where the necklace is still on my wrap on the sofa, glittering in the low light. Such an incredible piece of jewelry that has made headlines—and will again soon. Its edges seem a bit threatening. Or maybe I see a threat now that I never saw before.

I pick it up and hold the cold stones against my throat. Rock chips. Millions of years old. Why do these accidents of nature stir such passionate desire and greed, as opposed to other rocks and minerals? These stones, responsible for so much deception through so many centuries—all coming down to this moment, here and now, in the palazzo where I spent winter vacations as a child. I am part of their history now, for better or worse.

My father and I—we must be tainted. Something twisted inside us, a maligned trait. Like a family curse. And it's infecting Jerome, though he never asked for it. If I'm completely honest, I seduced him into it. I didn't mean to be cruel or misleading. I thought I was being sincere because I like him. Much more than I should. I offered him a choice. He agreed. But I wasn't sincere. Because he couldn't know how profound my desire for revenge runs. How much I'm willing to risk to prove the point. He might not have been so accommodating had he known. He might have told me what he said tonight—*you're nuts*—and run for the hills. For him, it would have been better. Probably for me, as well.

I'm still sorry for what I said. I could use the release we find in each other. And the reassurance that everything will go as planned.

I put the necklace on my bedside table, get under the sheets, turn off the lamp, and close my eyes. I can't think anymore.

When I wake, it feels as if it's only been a few minutes. But I must have fallen asleep right away, because while it's still dark outside, I'm wide-awake. I can usually sleep through the night, even when I'm anxious, the hazards of running a company where you can't let the strife interfere with your well-being, where you always have to be ready for battle. But looking at my watch on the bedside table, I see it's a little past four a.m.

What woke me?

Guilt. I think of Jerome down the hall in the guest room. We've not slept apart since this started. Not sex every night, of course, but most nights. I feel the emptiness of the bed like I've never felt it before—the solitude. I don't like it. I don't like missing someone in bed. It's dangerous. It's how it all starts. You start to depend. To rely. Then you need.

Still, I find myself getting up, pulling on my robe, belting it tightly as it as I leave my room and move down the hall to the guest room.

I pause for a moment before knocking. No answer.

"Jerome?"

He must be asleep. Will he mind me waking him? *Ania, it's Jerome. The man is a hound.* Smiling to myself, I open the door. The light is still on, the bed made. It doesn't look as if he's been here, just his open suitcase, his clothing jumbled and not yet unpacked. He scavenges for whatever he needs on the floor, though there's an antique bureau and closet. Does he think hangers and drawers are just for decoration?

And where is he?

Maybe still downstairs. Perhaps he decided to sulk on the sofa.

But everything is dark and quiet. He's not in the living room. I hear myself calling out his name and despise how it sounds, the plea in it. Wherever he is, he's not here. The house is empty. I make a cup of chamomile tea with a teaspoon of honey to take upstairs. I'll get back in bed and read for a while. Try not to worry. He was angry. He must have gone out. He doesn't know the city at all, so it could be hours until he makes his way back. Venice loves to ensnare visitors in her web. He's not going to like it, wandering around in circles until he has no choice but to ask for directions once it's light enough for someone to be around that he can stop. And with his Italian, or lack thereof—I suddenly laugh.

He's going to be boiling mad when he returns. I better be ready.

Returning to my bedroom, I put the tea on the bedside table and reach for my book.

And that's when I see what's wrong: the Thorne Lemon Twist.

It's gone.

Chapter 7

Jerome

Dawn in Venice. It's something to see. Even in winter. The fog burning off the canals, dissipating into fragments to veil the sunrise so everything turns an enchanted pink-gold. The city is like a mirage, the romantic fairy tale, picture-perfect for weddings and postcards.

Watching it from San Marco, the mosaics and the golden domes ablaze with sparkle, I think of how the sunlight must fall on Ania right now, curled in bed, her hair a tangled skein. Her fragrant smell of bath oil, of the after-musk of sex—

I can't. Moving back into the maze, I find myself walking into a café in the expensive district near San Marco with the shoe stores and cashmere shops, everything opening early to accommodate tourists here for Carnival, some already up, finishing their breakfasts and eager to brandish cameras and follow their guided tour pamphlets.

I must look as hungover as I feel. The surly man behind the café bar, framed by smoked hams hung on hooks with ribbons tied about the hooves as if a little festivity makes it less gruesome, gives me a look when I order a double espresso.

It helps. Not much, but the jolt of caffeine with two cubes of sugar clears my head somewhat of my funk. I light a cigarette and order another espresso. I'm delaying. I have to go back and talk to her. Or not talk to her, as the case might be. But I still have to face her. I should finish my second espresso and return before she wakes. Shower again. Try to look presentable. Not like I spent the night roaming aimlessly about Venice, brooding and asking myself if maybe this is the time to call it quits. Admit defeat.

Anyway, she's not one to care.

But I know she does. She just can't bring herself to say it. I know because when I have her in my arms, when I hear her gasp and see how she rocks upon me in abandon, her head thrown back—*that's* the Ania she hides from everyone else. The woman who doesn't want to be in control anymore. Who wants to lose herself. To be taken and to feel.

The problem is, the other Ania, the one from last night? She's all about control. Mistrust. Or maybe not mistrust as I see it, but stark refusal to rely on anyone but herself. She doesn't want to depend or ask for permission. To me, it's still mistrust. Not to her. Like the boutiques without price tags or no need for advance reservations—it's how she sees the world. What she's been taught. Her father's daughter.

And that's the Ania I can't deal with. I don't know her. I don't have the weapons to fight her. She draws that mantle of impenetrable frost around herself, and there's no getting inside. No windows. No door. Her heart sealed like a jewelry vault. All the beauty, the supple fragility, locked behind codes only she knows how to unlock.

What I've agreed to do, now that I really let myself see it—I must be crazy. It's not who I am. It goes against everything I believe in, what I fought against during the war and afterwards. I thought I wanted to catch the Leopard more than anything else. I thought I could do it. That *we* could do it together. But now that the hunt is on, I'm not so sure. Maybe I'm not made for this. I don't know how to steal. To lie. How to get away with it.

I can't make chitchat with a family friend with a stolen necklace in my wrist-bag.

Finishing the espresso, I take out my wallet and look in bewilderment at the lire notes. I don't even know how much money this is, for crying out loud. The bar guy doesn't seem to care. He keeps wiping down the stacked glasses on the counter as if he has all the time in the world to watch a hungover American try to figure out the price of his espressos.

I fumble in my jeans' pocket and locate some loose change, dumping it onto the counter with a clatter. The bar guy eyes me and starts to shift toward the coins suspiciously as if I've dropped a handful of bullets.

"*Due caffè latte, per favore,*" pipes an unexpected voice.

I turn. Lauren Segal, in beige slacks and a red flannel jacket with oversized buttons, a patterned scarf around her head. Face scrubbed clean. She looks prettier without the lipstick. Without the inferior emeralds. Younger. More like who she must be in real life. A California girl, friendly as summer beaches and hot dogs on the grill.

"Oh." She gives me a surprised look. "Fancy meeting you here."

"Yeah." My voice sounds like I slept on a sidewalk. "What are the odds?"

"After last night? Not much." She gestures to a table outside, where the old guy in the Napoleon hat from last night has his nose buried in a newspaper. "My dad. He likes to get up early. See the sights before it's crowded. You know?"

"Sure." I turn back to my indecipherable pile of coins, which the bar guy ignores as he prepares her order.

"Here." She steps to my side. "What did you have?"

"Two double espressos."

She asks the surly guy something in Italian then counts the coins— "Plus tip," she tells me. "They always expect a tip"—and slides the two coins left over to me. "First time here, huh?"

I nod gratefully and pocket the coins. Pause. What to say? I have to say something.

"Give me a sec." She goes outside to deliver her father's latte and returns to me. I light another cigarette.

"Can I bum one?" She glances askance at her dad, who hasn't looked up from his paper.

I offer the crumpled pack and light one for her. She draws in, exhales with vigor. "Ah."

"He doesn't let you smoke?" She's certainly old enough.

"He doesn't like it." She scrunches up her nose. "You'd think running a studio in Hollywood—everyone smokes. Hours loitering on the set, waiting for a camera or lighting fix. What else is there to do? Smoke or gossip. Usually, both."

"Sounds..."

"Boring." She takes another vigorous inhale. "Everyone thinks making movies is so exciting. Like costume balls in Venice. It's not. Well. Except for last night."

I feel uncomfortable, like my guilt is branded on my mug. "That was something else, wasn't it?"

She laughs. "You got off easy. I've barely slept a wink. That inspector had us there for hours. Questioning us one by one."

"You, too?"

"Sure." She eyes me. "I was there, wasn't I? It wasn't so bad. Not for me."

"Why?"

"I know your name now." A sly but not malicious smile.

"Really. How?"

"The inspector. He asked if I knew you. If I'd seen you around. You know, like I said. Everyone knows everyone else. Small circle."

A prickle of unease creeps through me. "What did you tell him?" Then, thinking this might sound suspicious—why should I care what she said?—I add, "I mean, he didn't ask us much. Just when I danced with Julie. For how long. Stuff like that."

"I told him I met you at the party." She rubs out the cigarette in the tin ashtray on the counter. "We talked. I liked you." She fusses with her scarf. "The truth."

"Oh. Right. Well, it was nice to see you again." I start awkwardly to the café door.

"Hey."

I turn and look at her.

"Don't be a stranger. It's a beautiful city. The Italians, they don't like it if you don't speak the language, but just tip them enough, and they get over it. Money is international. Everyone understands it."

All of a sudden, I want to tell her everything. The candor in her voice. No evasion. No ulterior motive to decipher. Just friendly California. What you see is what you get.

"I wish I could stay and chat, but…"

"Sure." She waves her hand. "I have to get back to my father anyway. Museums and churches. Yawn. Maybe another time."

"I'd like that." I hear myself say it and realize I actually mean it.

"We're staying at the Danieli. Leave me a message. Or ask for me. I'm here for two weeks. Museums and churches, plus more parties. Dad has to get his money's worth."

I feel myself smile. "Boring."

"You got that right." She winks. "But not so boring if I can see you."

When I reach the palazzo, I stop and take out the last cigarette from the pack. I forgot to buy more. Money might be international, but facing another dour shopkeeper waiting for me to hand over the right amount for a pack of Lucky Strikes is too much for me right now. I must have an extra pack somewhere in my suitcase.

I smoke and watch the climbing sun melt away the night from the palazzo's red brick façade. Brick and marble. In a city that floods annually, built on marshlands.

The sheer defiance of it.

Then I steel myself and use the key to go inside, moving to the staircase. Suddenly, Ania calls out from the living room. "Jerome?"

At the entryway, I see her in a white cloth robe. Barefoot. Her hair an untidy knot, tendrils falling about her face. It looks as if she hasn't gotten much sleep either. She has bruised circles under her eyes.

The tangled skein. The morning light...

I can't breathe again.

"Where were you?" Accusatory. Not soft or open to abandon.

"Taking a walk. Why? Do I need to ask permission? You certainly don't."

Her mouth tightens. A thin smile. "A walk. At this hour?"

"No. At the hour you told me you wanted to be alone."

"All night?" Dubious, as if she has any right.

"Yes. All night. Or what was left of it. Is there a problem?"

"I don't know." She moves to the sofa, pauses there. "Depends on what you did."

"I didn't do anything. I walked. Smoked. Had a coffee at a café. Make that two coffees. I have a splitting headache. So, if you don't mind, I'll take myself upstairs to shower and—"

As I turn away, her voice comes at me, a blade at my back. "Where is it?"

I halt and turn back around to her. "What?"

"The necklace." She pulls her wrap from the sofa, shakes it. Lets it flutter to the floor.

For a second, I can't speak. "What do you mean, where is it?"

She stares at me. "Exactly what I said. What did you do with it?"

"Do? I didn't—"

"I get it. You think I don't, but I do." Her voice is hard, as if she's had all this time to think and reach an inarguable conclusion. "The war.

What you saw. It changed you. I can't claim to know. I wasn't there. I didn't see any of it. Only the newsreels. But it happened. It happened to so many. How can you not feel as if you must stand for something better? Be someone better?"

"Ania, what is this all about?" My mind is whirling, trying to connect the dots.

She paces to the window to gaze out on the vista, so familiar to her. Her childhood playground. Vacations in Italy. "I thought you wanted this. I really did. I thought you wanted to catch him."

I take a tentative step toward her. "I thought I did, too."

"So that's why?" She keeps her eyes on the view but she's not seeing it. She's looking much farther away, to somewhere I can't travel. "Did you return it to her palazzo? Leave it on the doorstep or shove it through the mail slot? Or to the police station, a plain envelope left on the receptionist desk? Gabrielli will see it delivered. He'll be relieved. All the work. The investigation. The interruption during Carnival. No one likes to make too much effort here."

I suddenly understand. "You think I took it? To give it back?"

She whirls to me. "If not you, then who?"

"Ania. It has to be here. I didn't touch it. I went out, that's all." I turn to the sofa, stepping over her crumpled wrap. Overturn the cushions. Get on my knees to peer underneath, swiping my palms across the floorboards. There isn't a speck of dust.

"I already looked," she says. "I searched everywhere."

"But…it has to be here. What about the staff? Have you asked them? Maybe they found it and put it away for safety—" Even as I say this, my stomach plunges. If someone other than us saw it here, they could recognize it once it's all over the newspapers. Put two and two together. Call the police.

"It's six-fifteen in the morning. The housekeeper and cook aren't live-in. They arrive at seven-thirty. They couldn't have taken it."

"Well, someone did," I reply, sharply enough to make her pause.

"You really didn't…?" She suddenly appears frightened.

"Of course, not. Ania, I don't like how it went down. I don't like how—but I'm not an idiot. I'm not going to risk trying to return it. It never crossed my mind."

Her face, if possible, turns whiter. Almost translucent. "Well, it's not here."

"Are you sure? I mean, one hundred percent certain?"

"Yes." A flash of anger. "I've looked everywhere. I took a bath. I came downstairs and took it. Put it on my nightstand. I went to bed. Then I woke up and felt—never mind what I felt. I saw you hadn't slept in the guest room. I thought maybe you stayed here instead."

"On that Louis XIV sofa? After our night of debauchery and pillage?"

She grimaces. "You weren't here. I made a cup of tea, went back upstairs, and saw the necklace was gone. I thought—"

"I know what you thought. It wasn't me. I swear it."

She drops onto the sofa as if she's lost the strength to stay upright. Her fingers graze the upholstery in small circles like she might unearth it from the unyielding fabric.

She looks up to meet my baffled stare. "Someone must have taken it. From us."

And then the door chime rings.

Los Angeles Daily News. January 5, 1959

Oh, my dovelies. SCANDAL! Yours truly, Tattle-Dove, is in Venice. We can't say much for the weather. It's not summer in Cannes, but the city is divine. You simply have to be here.

But the ball of the season at Casa d'Maglione did *not* go as expected. Oh, everyone who is anyone was there. You couldn't trip without bumping into a famous face. And the contessa was sublime in black Balenciaga and her vintage Thorne necklace. You know the one, the rare yellow diamond her doting husband gave her on their engagement. Let me tell you, no one had anything to equal it. Not even Ania Thorne, who was at the ball with a very mysterious stranger from our own U.S of A.

Now, brace yourselves, dovelies. There was a crime! The contessa's necklace was stolen from her bedroom mid-gaiety. Imagine the uproar. Why, it was Hiroshima for high society.

And while no one can say it aloud because it's an active investigation, the police found a glove: the calling card of that notorious thief known as the Leopard, who's made off with a substantial pile of loot over the years and has never been caught. Everyone is beside themselves. We won't see a jewel in public until Christmas. I'm on the case. So, wish me luck. And stay tuned to this page. We have so much to tattle about. Ta-ta for now!

Chapter 8

Ania

Jerome spins around as if he heard a gunshot.

"Go upstairs," I tell him. "Take your shower. Put on some decent clothes, please."

"Who—who can it be?" he stammers. He looks terrible. I again feel that twinge of regret for having been such a bitch. It wasn't enough to kick him out of my bed. I then had to accuse him of taking the necklace. I can see by his expression that he's at his wits' end. He doesn't know how to contend with any of this. With me. But he has to pull it together for both our sakes. He can't afford to fall apart now. Neither of us can.

"Go." I stab my hand toward the stairs. He bolts out of the living room.

The doorbell rings again, insistently. I'm barefoot. I must look a fright. I twist my hair up into a hasty chignon, tighten the robe at my waist, and pad into the foyer, wincing at the chill of the marble under my feet. No time to go to my bedroom to fetch slippers. Whoever is at the palazzo isn't making a social call at six-thirty in the morning on a Sunday in Venice.

When I open the door, I have to repress my dismay.

Gabrielli. In the same suit he wore the other night. He removes his hat and gives the dip of his head I've known since I was a girl, always so well-mannered, even if he looks as if he only owns the one suit. So polite, so Venetian. One of the things my father most loved about coming here—how civilized it is. He always said Venice was a world apart. A place where time moved more slowly, and people remembered that not everything in life was about money and success.

I force out smile. "*Commissario*. What a surprise."

"Signorina Thorne." He makes a contrite gesture. "Did I wake you? Unforgivable, I know. But…"

"No, no." I open the door wider and step aside. "Please, come in."

"Are you certain? I don't wish to intrude."

"I was already awake. Still on American time. The staff isn't here."

"Oh." He pauses. "Just for a moment, yes?"

"Of course." I escort him into the living room. He doesn't take a seat. He stands there holding his hat, waiting for my invitation. Civilized. Like the world used to be.

"Please, sit down." Do I sound nervous? I don't hear it in my voice. "If you'll allow me a few minutes, I just need to dress. Then I'll make some coffee. Would you like coffee?"

The offer is ingrained in me. One of my mother's lessons. Regardless of whether one has help or not, you always offer personally. You don't wait for the butler to do it. You assume command of your household because that's how you'll be taken seriously.

"*Café, sí.*" He nods. "If it's not too much trouble."

"Not at all. Please, make yourself at home. I'll just be a moment."

I make sure I depart slowly, not in any rush. A woman tired from the evening's events, up early because of jet lag but not at all concerned to find the family friend, the *commissario* no less, on her doorstep at this ungodly hour. Once I reach the landing upstairs, I stop to press a hand to my chest.

My heart is racing. But not like last night when I stole the necklace.

I hear the shower running in the guest bathroom. I hesitate. I don't want to throw him into a panic, but he has to know. I've an uneasy feeling that Gabrielli isn't here for a social call. And I have to change, make my way to the kitchen, and put the espresso pot on the stove. Set up a tray. Act as if this unexpected development is ordinary. The staff isn't coming in today. It's Sunday. No one except those who make a living off tourism work on Sundays in Venice.

And Gabrielli. Evidently, he works on Sundays, too.

Stepping into the tiled bathroom, I avert my eyes from the sight of Jerome, naked and too tall for the stall, hirsute and wiry with muscle. His body is a sculpture, marred by his scars, the chips and dents of his service during the war. He's beautiful to me because of it. Not perfect. But perfect anyway. The kind of man I never thought I'd be attracted to—too coarse along the edges, too feral and inescapable like a wolf.

"It's Gabrielli," I say.

He turns, soap suds sliding down his ridged abdomen. "Here?"

I nod, still keeping my eyes averted but not enough. I want to throw off my robe and join him. It's absurd. We were just arguing, and the police inspector is waiting in the living room. How can I want to make love to him now, in a shower too small for both of us?

"Christ." He shifts to let the water run down his back. "Did he say why?"

"No." I force myself to turn away to face the bathroom door. "Whatever it is, Jerome, don't say more than he asks. Okay? Just stay calm."

"Yeah. Okay." He blinks, soap in his eyes. A question. Fear.

I don't stay. I don't reassure him. I can't lie to him again.

Chapter 9

Jerome

What to wear when the police arrive to question you? I stand with a towel knotted around my waist, staring down at my upended suitcase. For the life of me, I have no idea. Jeans? Khakis? Dress trousers? I have two pairs of the first, two of the second, one of the third. And I don't like the third. Wool. They itch. Have pleats.

The sound of her footsteps comes down the corridor, pauses at the doorway.

"You're still not dressed?"

I look up at her, feeling a smile twisting my mouth. "I don't know what to wear."

She sighs and steps into the room. I smell her perfume as she starts to bend over the suitcase. She's changed into a black top and sleek, black pants that hug her long legs and end above her ankles. Ballet flats. Her hair is pulled back from her face in her signature bun. Very light lipstick. She still looks tired, but...wow. Also stunning.

I lurch forward and haul the suitcase onto the bed, grappling with my towel. Don't want to give her another peep show. I saw how she eyed me in the shower. Gotta say, it made me feel very manly for the short time it lasted, a reminder that I still catch her attention. Maybe I should just walk around naked for the rest of our stay.

She picks through my things. "Honestly," she mutters. "What is all this?"

"My clothes," I say.

She turns, my favorite black turtleneck in her hand. The one I wore in Paris. The one she wore after we—

"This," she says. "Jeans and loafers. No socks."

"No socks?"

"Like you slept here. Casual. You're not worried, Jerome." She lays the turtleneck on the bed. "We're not worried. Right?"

"Right." I nod.

She goes to the door. "I have to make him some coffee. Just go down and talk to him. Act normal. We've nothing to hide. We're willing to cooperate. Why wouldn't we be?"

"Sure. Why wouldn't we?" I meet her eyes. She looks away. Walks away.

I get dressed and run a brush over my hair. Too short. Makes me feel like I'm back in the army, in the trenches, lice scampering over my scalp as I wait for a Nazi bomb to blow me to pieces. Then I waste time searching my suitcase for cigarettes, grit embedded at the bottom of those little side pockets that don't hold anything bigger than a tie. Ah-ha. Here they are. The last pack, bent and stuffed into a shoe. But intact.

Nicotine. I'm going to need it.

The inspector sits on the sofa with his hat beside him like an Italian version of Sam Spade. If Sam Spade had put on thirty pounds of spaghetti dinners and lost most of his hair. He comes to his feet at my entrance. A courteous offer of his hand.

"Ah. Signor Curtis. My apologies for the intrusion. You slept well?"

"Yeah." I shake his hand. Firm. Not moist like last night. A man in charge now.

"No—how do you say it? Jet lag?" he asks.

"I never get it." Then, thinking I've already made a blunder, I ask, "Why?"

"No reason." He gives me a curious smile.

"I was in the army," I explain, turning to a chair. Make myself sit. Act normal. Nothing to hide. Willing to cooperate. I light a cigarette, though Ania hates it indoors. Screw it. She can berate me later, make that disgusted face and fling open the windows, complaining about the stink. "I had to learn to sleep anywhere. At any time."

"Oh. The army. The Allies?"

I nod, drawing in a lungful of smoke. Then I remember and extend the pack to him.

"No. *Grazie.*" He lifts a hand. "I had to give it up. The signora, my wife, she doesn't like it." A moment of contemplation. A slight lean toward me. "Maybe just one."

I chuckle and click my butane lighter for him. "That's how it starts. Just one."

"Yes." He draws on the cigarette with a hearty sigh. "I miss it."

I wait. He's not here to smoke with me.

"The Allies. You were here? In Italy? During the war?"

"Yes. First here, then France. Afterwards, Germany."

"Germany. You saw...?"

"I did." I hear the tightness in my voice, take another drag to hide it.

"Terrible time." He shakes his head. "Terrible. The years don't make it better."

"Not for some," I say.

"You?"

"I'm okay." I force out a smile that feels wrong on my face. "It's been a long time."

"But still. No jet lag. Sleep anywhere. Anytime."

"You know what they say. Once a soldier..." I lean back. Then realize there's no ashtray nearby. I tap ash into my palm and rub it into my jeans. When I see him staring, I say, "Army trick."

"Ah." He looks amused, but he gets up and goes to the mantel over the fireplace, fetching a crystal receptacle that looks as if it was made for displaying fruit or something.

He sets it on the circular table between us. "Murano," he says. He crushes out his cigarette in it. Didn't take more than a few hits.

"The famous glass of Venice?" he says, noticing my silence. "No?"

"First time here. Sorry."

"Oh, you must go and see." The proud Venetian. Offering assistance to the new *Americano* in town. "Exquisite craftsmanship. An entire island for glassmaking."

"Huh." I guess that thing's probably way too expensive to use as an ashtray, but I do so anyway. What the hell?

"First time in Venezia?" He pauses. "There's never another first time."

"It's nice," I say. When he looks surprised, I add, "Very beautiful."

"But cold, yes? In the summer, too hot. In the winter, cold and wet."

Am I supposed to say something about the weather?

"Signorina Thorne knows Venice very well," he goes on. "She's an honorary citizen."

"Yes." Now, I feel him inching toward the gist of it. "Her family. She told me. Used to come here every year for Carnival."

"You know her family?"

I hesitate. "Not really."

"No?"

"We haven't—" I start to pull out another cigarette and stop myself. I don't want to look nervous. "It's not the right time yet."

"Ah." An understanding nod. The man of the world again. "Too soon."

"Yes. Too soon." Where the hell is Ania with the coffee?

"You met her…?"

"In France," I say carefully. I don't know what else to say. We didn't coordinate our stories. Didn't discuss what happens if we're questioned. It never occurred to us that we might be. Another oversight of mine. A mistake. I should have prepared. I used to do this man's job, after all. I know the guidelines for finding the culprit.

The hired help as her date…

"France." He sticks out his lower lip as if the answer's not pleasing to him.

"Yes. Cannes."

"Ah. The film festival. Marvelous."

"If you like that sort of thing." I feel as if I'm hanging over a cliff.

Then she appears with a tray. Coffee cups, a china pot. Sugar. Cream. A plate of—

"Biscotti," Gabrielli exclaims. "Signorina Thorne, too much trouble."

"Not at all." Ania sets the tray on the table. Doesn't glance at the Murano bowl with the smoldering cigarette butts. "I'm sorry I can't offer anything more. We only just arrived. The staff hasn't fully stocked the kitchen yet."

"No, no." He crunches on a biscotti as she serves his coffee. I'm amazed. Who knew? I'm so used to seeing her being served; it's strange to see how hospitable she is. How gracious, like she serves coffee and biscotti to rumpled police inspectors every day.

She sits on the other end of the sofa, her legs crossed. I notice her wrap is still there, draped over the side.

"Signor Curtis was telling me about Cannes," Gabrielli says, taking up his coffee cup.

She doesn't look at me, but I feel it anyway. A furtive stab of her eyes.

"Cannes," she repeats calmly. "Yes."

"Where we met," I add.

"Yes." She smiles. "At the film festival."

Gabrielli makes a little sound of appreciation as he tastes the coffee. "When?" he asks, smiling at her. "Espresso. Like an Italian."

"Nine months ago," she replies. "I was there on business."

"Almost a year." He sounds surprised.

I wince inside. Is almost a year enough time to meet the family?

He lets uncomfortable silence settle, sipping his espresso and munching on his biscotti until he looks up, slightly perturbed. "You don't?"

"Oh." I immediately start to stand, but Ania is quicker, pouring me a cup and handing it to me. Then she takes the sugar bowl and adds two cubes to my cup. Familiar with how I take my coffee. Gabrielli, I see, takes note of it.

"None for me," she says, sitting back down. "I'll have some tea later."

"I intrude," he says, apologetic.

"Of course, not." Ania smiles. "It's no trouble at all."

"It is." He lets another silence ensue. The coffee wreaks havoc on my nerves. My third espresso. I'm going to be jumping around like a gazelle after this. Forget getting any sleep, though I desperately need it.

"I must do my duty." Again apologetic as if his duty is distasteful. Poor manners.

"Naturally," says Ania. "We understand."

"I'm afraid I must ask for Signor Curtis's passport."

"Excuse me?" I blurt out.

"Paperwork." He sighs. "Routine. I'm so sorry."

"Wait a minute." I put down my cup. Ania stares at me. "Why my passport?"

He gives a regretful smile. "A few days only. Yes? You stay for Carnival?" He looks over at Ania, who nods. "Two weeks. A few days is nothing. I return it before you go."

"But..." I feel my jaw clench. "I don't understand why."

He doesn't answer. He doesn't have to.

"Fine." I stand and move to the entryway. Gabrielli reaches for the last piece of biscotti, and I hear Ania ask, "Would you like more?" His reply, "No, signorina. So kind. I intrude."

Upstairs, I bang my knee against the bedside table and curse under my breath as I search my suitcase. I find my passport in a side pocket. Flipping it open, I quickly search the pages. The stamps. It doesn't contain any of my service entries or departures. I got a new passport when I moved to London. My green card form is glued to the inside back cover.

He wants my passport. Routine. Paperwork. Why?

He's already in the foyer when I descend. I hand it to him.

"I take good care," he says as if I'm worried that he'll lose it. "Just routine."

"Routine." I'm too angry now to mind my tone.

"Yes. So sorry. An inconvenience, I know." He chats with Ania in Italian. *Arrivederci*. Murano. Is he offering her tour advice, for chrissakes?

When he finally leaves, and she shuts the door, I can't keep the fury from my voice. "He took my goddamn passport. Just like I told you. All of us at the party. He's trapping us here. No one leaves Venice until he says so."

She says quietly, "Not all of us."

"What?"

"Only you. He took your passport. Not mine." She moves past me back into the living room and starts gathering the tray. The soiled ashtray. "Crack open those terrace doors, will you? All this smoke in here."

"Fuck the smoke."

She goes still. "Jerome, it's not—"

"The hell it's not. It's my passport." I seize my cigarettes and light one, deliberately, without cracking open the terrace doors.

She harrumphs, opens the terrace doors herself, and then returns to the tray.

"Aren't you going to say anything?" I hear my resentment, the jagged edge of too much caffeine. The accusation. As if she suspected this might happen and kept me in the dark on purpose.

"What do you want me to say? I'm not going to fly into a panic because he took your passport. He said it was routine. He's probably only doing it because he doesn't know you. He wants to see if your story checks out."

"He asked Lauren Segal about me."

She pauses. "How do you know?"

"Because I ran into her this morning at a café. By chance. He kept everyone but us there for hours, questioning all of them. It's what I'd do. Question everyone in the heat of the moment while they're still in shock, then go back to each of them later to see if their stories change. If they make a mistake."

"And you didn't think to tell me?"

"I didn't think it mattered. But he asked her if she knew me. If she'd seen me around. So, it's not routine. He has me in his sights."

"You didn't think it mattered? With Gabrielli at our front door?" She starts toward the kitchen, carrying the tray with me right behind her.

"No. I didn't think it mattered. Why would I?"

"Because Julie's necklace was stolen." She sets the tray on the granite kitchen counter with more force than necessary, making the cups rattle. "Jerome, if he asked Lauren Segal about you last night, of course it matters. Especially if he then comes here first thing in the morning to confiscate your passport. You should have told me."

"I didn't know he was going to confiscate my passport. Did you?"

She gives me an incredulous stare. "You seem to think this is some plot against you. We did it together, remember? If you get caught, I get caught."

"Really?" I don't want to say it. I know I shouldn't. I do it anyway. "He didn't confiscate your passport, Signorina Thorne. The honorary citizen. Friend of the family. But me, I'm the stranger. *Small circle*, Lauren said. Everyone knows everyone. Except me."

"You were dancing with Julie." Her voice is taut. She's angry, too, but God forbid she should just explode and let me have it. "Everyone saw you with her. He might have you in his sights for now because of the small circle, but he can't—he *won't*—find anything. There's nothing to find."

"Except the stolen necklace we don't have anymore. There's that to find."

She takes a moment before saying, "I suppose you think that's my fault, too."

I don't answer. She walks around me to the kitchen door. "You need to get some sleep. You're frustrated and upset—"

"Can you blame me? We stole a necklace that's somehow gone missing. My passport just got taken by the police. Don't I have the right to be pissed off?"

"You do." She doesn't look at me. "But you have to sleep. You can't do anything in this state. You'll only make it worse."

"What about you?"

She takes another moment. "I'm going out."

"Out?"

"Yes. To do some shopping. See if I can have lunch with someone he kept there for hours last night. If Lauren Segal felt free to talk, so will the others. If only out of morbid curiosity. Small circle. I know them all. They'll tell me if I ask."

"And you think that's smart? To ask about the commissario over lunch?"

"People in my circle like to talk. It's what we do, didn't you know? Look at Lauren Segal. A chance meeting in a café, and she spills the beans. And it was my father's necklace. His design. They'll be desperate to get my take on it. So, yes, it's a smart move. We have to know what's being said. What they said to him."

"What they might be saying about me," I add darkly.

"That, too." She fixes me with her stare. "Get some sleep, Jerome. I can't have you falling apart. We have to find that necklace. Before Gabrielli does. And I need you at your best. We can't do this without you at your best."

"Sure. All right. I'll get some sleep."

"There are sleeping pills in my bathroom," she says. "Take one. I mean it."

Chapter 10

Ania

After changing into a pair of loose black slacks, a cashmere pullover, a billowing white Dior coat, and a cashmere scarf, I feel almost like myself again. As if it's one of those rare days when I have time to myself to browse the shops and have a leisurely lunch. Not worried about the business or the new line. Not concerned about a stolen necklace.

I walk confidently into the maze of streets and alleyways. I know Venice well after years of visiting. I still wish I could get lost sometimes. Like when it was mysterious to me—a young girl whose life up until then had been skyscrapers and penthouses, crowded streets, and barrages of traffic. Venice, like a fairy realm—eerily hushed, mystical, and full of hidden places waiting for me to explore. The constant susurration of water, my mother's warnings to be careful, to not trip and fall, that the canals could be deceptively deep—it fascinated me. I fantasized about falling into the water and drifting down to a secret kingdom inhabited by mermaids and seahorses, pearl castles, and chests full of gemstones waiting to be made into jewelry.

I eventually learned it's not the water that protects Venice. It's the silt, the mud. The man-made layers in the canals and ridges in the lagoon that break the tides and keep them from washing the city away. Just ordinary mud.

Then, I grew older. It's still a beautiful place to visit, but no longer my fairy realm.

As I reach San Marco, I pause, still uncertain if I'm doing the right thing. But as I stroll through the glass doors of the Danieli and walk to the concierge, I know I don't have a lot of choices. This is my chance if I want to find out what happened after we left Julie's palazzo.

"Mr. Hugh Lockling," I tell the uniformed man on duty. "Please say it's Ania Thorne."

"Certainly, Signorina Thorne."

While I wait, I survey the lobby. I catch sight of a weary-looking Lauren Segal with an older man, going into the hotel restaurant. Her father, Lionel Segal, of Segal Pictures. He courted us like a lover, dangling loads of cash to get us to loan him jewels for a movie with a new starlet he hoped to launch to fame. Our insurance company balked at the risk. We couldn't do it, even if we'd wanted to. And my father didn't. He said he designed and sold jewelry to movie stars because it was a necessity. They were photographed in it, bolstering our cachet. But a credit on a picture? The chaos on a set, where anything could be misplaced or lost? Bah, he grimaced. So vulgar. Later on, he said the same—and worse—about the movie stars who thought they didn't have to pay their bills.

I turn my back to the lobby. Lauren Segal and her father are the last people I want to spot me here. Or be obliged to talk to.

The concierge hands me the phone.

"Ania?" Hugh says. "To what do I owe this surprise?"

"You said we should have lunch, didn't you? Do you have plans?"

"Nothing I can't cancel. Meet me in the restaurant in ten minutes."

"I'll walk over to Harry's and meet you there. Better drinks," I say. "Better crowd."

"Okay." A pause. "I don't care about the crowd. You're the only person I want to see."

"But I have to see who else is there. Take your time. I'll order you a Bellini."

He laughs. "You remember."

The maître d' at Harry's has been here since my parents married and knows me like I know Venice. He greets me warmly and shows me to a table by the window. I settle into the low, leather-cushioned chair. This has always been one of my favorite places in the world, with its flattering lighting and crisp peach-colored linens, the finest food in the city, if a place only foreigners can appreciate. I let the atmosphere wash over me and feel my nerves quiet. Before I can ask, the waiter places a flute before me—a mixture of cold peach nectar and champagne, along with a plate of wafer-thin zucchini rounds, fried and lightly salted. Next comes the bread basket—warm, flaky rolls wrapped in more crisp peach linen.

I take a sip of the cocktail. My anxiety ebbs. I can do this. I'm my father's daughter. He had a first time, too. There must have been a learning curve for him, as well. But I'm a quick study. Papa always said that. He isn't here to teach me, so I have to learn as I go. Like I learned to run the company. He never taught me much about that. He prepared me, but he always assumed I'd take over when he was ready, a slow transition that he'd oversee, never being completely out of the picture. He was wrong. And I figured it out. I learned on my own.

I hope this lunch will prove useful. Hugh's father and Julie's husband are friends, and I expect Hugh only helped her deal with her loss last night out of obligation. No doubt, at some point in the past, she made a play for him, too, like she made a play for Jerome at her party. She's like that. To her, sexual conquests are rungs to a better spot on the marquee. You can take the girl out of Hollywood, but not the Hollywood out of the girl.

"Ania." Hugh leans down to kiss me on my cheek. Despite the winter chill, he's in a light wool suit and brought in some cold air with him. I feel it on my skin and pull my cashmere scarf tighter around my throat, meeting his eyes.

He sits. The waiter brings him a Bellini.

"To old times and new beginnings." He holds up his glass. I touch mine to his.

We sip. I look at him from under my lashes, curious, and he gives me a sidelong glance. Our old body language. Familiar. It actually feels good, reassuring that at least one thing remains the same. Something I can count on.

"I'm surprised," he says. "Delighted, but surprised. You seemed uncertain about meeting up when I suggested it at the party."

"Yes, well, that was at the party. I was caught off guard by a lot of things."

"I can imagine. Are you all right?"

"Not really." I pause, hoping I look concerned. "It's why I wanted to see you. I feel like...I had the wind knocked out of me."

"I know. It was quite frightening. Everyone was knocked out by it. But I have to ask, what about the schlub?"

I feel an immediate rise in tension. "He has a name."

"Do I have to use it? He's not going to be around long enough for us to become buddies, is he?"

The confidence. Hugh never lacked it. I once found it so attractive. It reminded me of my father. Like there wasn't anything in the world he couldn't accomplish—or take as his.

He smiles. "I know you, Ania. As well as anyone does."

"People change."

"Not really. They might do things differently. But they don't change. You're Ania Thorne. An incredible designer. A formidable businesswoman. A man like that—I suppose he's a diversion, but hardly a long-term commitment."

Anger burns in me. I have to keep it under control. "You're making a lot of assumptions."

"Am I? I guess he deserves a break. Shouldn't speak ill of the dead."

"What?" I'm startled. "Whatever do you mean by that?"

"Well, everyone thinks he did it. The outsider. They're placing bets."

"Who else is in the running?" I ask, taking the last sip of my drink and immediately wanting something else. Hugh notices and orders a bottle of wine. I know I should refuse, but I'm nervous again. And it's Italy. Wine with lunch. It's ordinary. Expected.

"The hired help, I suppose. Though I doubt they did it. Maybe those who were guests of guests. But the schlub is leading the pack. That inspector made that pretty obvious."

"He did?"

"Oh, I forgot. You left early. He didn't let us leave early. Kept asking us the same questions over and over, then circling back to Julie." He chuckles. "She was mad as a hornet. She told him if he didn't find her necklace, she would call a press conference. A *press conference*, can you believe it? The inspector wasn't amused. He warned her that talking to reporters wouldn't help the case."

"What did he keep asking her?" I hear my voice. Not a waver. Not a tremor. Idle conversation over lunch with wine.

"About the necklace. The bodyguard. He said the bodyguard saw someone sneak upstairs. The inspector was all over that. But the bodyguard wasn't sure what he saw, and you know Julie. Too much to drink. She couldn't remember exactly when she went upstairs. And none of us ever saw the bodyguard before the necklace was stolen. It got tiresome."

"Did he ask you any questions?"

Hugh laughs. "Yes. Had I ever met your schlub? Did I know anything about him?"

The waiter arrives to take our orders. The veal for Hugh. Dover sole for me.

"So, he asked about Jerome?" I say casually as he pours us more wine.

"Pretty much. And the big question after you left was: How well do you know the guy?"

"How well do *I* know him? He was my date."

"Ania." Hugh gives me a look as if he's still in tune with my private life. "Listen. I get it. You're at the top of your game. Head of the company now. It must get lonely. He's good-looking enough, I suppose. But really, how well do you know him?"

"Well enough to know he's not a thief. Just because he's not part of our tribe doesn't mean he's a criminal."

"I didn't say that."

"Actually, you did. You said everyone is placing bets on it. Is Gabrielli placing bets? Or does he have some evidence to back it up?"

Hugh takes a moment. I have to be careful. He sees himself as the superior man. Jerome isn't someone he'd ever consider as competition. I have to make light of the relationship while still defending Jerome. I can't make it seem as if I'm too invested.

"Other than the glove?" he says at length. "Not that he mentioned. But it's a man's glove, after all. Fits the pattern of all those heists that have been going on for years. And it was the *L.A. Daily* this morning. That silly Tattle-Dove column."

"It was?"

"Yep. Tattle-Dove claims it was the Leopard, for whatever that's worth."

I don't reveal the knot his name rouses in my chest. "Be that as it may, they can't go around accusing someone just because they don't know him. The Leopard didn't attend the parties of any of the women he stole from, as far as I know."

Hugh pauses again. "Do you know?"

"Know what?" I force myself to fork a piece of my sole. Eat it before it gets cold.

"About the Leopard. That incident in Cannes. It was all over the newspapers, too. Then it wasn't. Did they ever catch the guy who stole your collection?"

"No," I say shortly. "They never said it was the Leopard, either."

"But it could have been?"

I have to nod. "Yes. But again, no evidence. Like last night."

"Outside of the glove. So. Why are you interested? I mean, besides the fact that your father designed the necklace."

I curb my exasperation. "I'm interested because they're placing bets on an innocent man. And Gabrielli confiscated Jerome's passport," I say, realizing I can't avoid it. "If everyone thinks he did it without evidence, how is that fair? What people say matters. Did Gabrielli take anyone else's passport?"

"No. Why would he?" He reaches out for my hand. "Ania, please tell me you aren't seriously involved with this guy. I can deal with you asking me to lunch to grill me for his sake, but I'm worried he might be using you."

"*Using* me?" My voice rises a notch. "I'm not Julie. Not some damsel in distress in need of rescue from the big bad wolf."

He laughs again. "Heaven forbid. Ania Thorne, damsel in distress. Call that press conference." His mirth fades. "I'm just saying, if you don't know the guy well, maybe he's not who you think he is. If he stole the Lemon Twist, you could be in danger."

"And I'm telling you, he didn't steal it."

"Is he staying with you at the palazzo?"

I don't answer.

"Ania, let me book you a room at the Danieli. I can keep an eye on you."

I look up. "Thank you. I'm fine. I don't believe for a second that Jerome is guilty." Nor do I need anyone keeping an eye on me.

"Really? Well, I don't like the way you say his name."

I have to meet his stare. Need to play this right. I have to make sure he believes me and has no doubts about my intentions.

"You don't need to worry. Jerome was in the army. He fought the Germans. He's a good man. He couldn't possibly come up with a plot to steal a dozen eggs, let alone Julie's necklace. Let's not talk about him anymore. We're here together, after all this time. I could use your support right now."

"You're right. Enough about the schlub. You must be devastated. Almost as much as Julie. She couldn't stop wailing. Have you called your father?"

"No. I wouldn't know how to tell him. He wanted that necklace returned for our archives, and Julie refused. To have it stolen... He'll be beside himself."

"I can imagine. First Cannes, now this. I'm worried about you, darling."

After we finish, Hugh insists on paying the check and invites me to take a walk. I accept. There's no reason to say no. Jerome is sleeping, and if I continue with Hugh, I might get more information, something that might actually help me figure out what to do next.

We walk along the Grand Canal, stop for coffee, go into shops. In one that stocks lovely, marbleized papers and notebooks, I let Hugh buy me small journal bound in peacock-colored leather. He then pulls me into a jewelry shop and insists on buying me a diamond-encrusted Carnival mask pendant on a gold chain, saying we have to celebrate our reunion. So confident. As if the celebration is our first inevitable step toward reconciliation. A bauble to cement his determination. Jerome already forgotten, not worth his time.

It's almost too easy to slip back into the pattern of our past as the afternoon light fades and the temperature dips. But then it's suddenly past four, and I realize it's getting late. I have to get back to the palazzo. Jerome and I need to talk. Decide what to do. Figure out our next step. I have to help him out of this mess I've put him in. Because, of course, it's my fault. I thought I planned it so perfectly.

Until I didn't.

Hugh offers to walk me back to the palazzo, but I insist that he leave me at the stairs at the Ponte dei Carmini. After a few minutes of arguing about the encroaching dark and my safety, both of which I brush aside, he makes me promise to have dinner with him when we're both back in New York. He's leaving tomorrow for Milan on a business trip. But he clearly isn't going to give up on me, and it isn't an easy promise for me to make. I hate making vows I don't intend to keep, and I don't think there's any chance I'll be keeping this one. He hasn't provided much in the way of information—and isn't likely to. Whatever he knows is just gossip gleaned from the other guests, all of whom have evidently decided that Jerome is responsible. It's how they do things. So unpleasant. Therefore, accuse the person no one cares about or thinks they'll see again and move on.

I don't know if I should feel reassured or saddened as I watch Hugh walk away towards the Danieli. A time, not long ago, I might have jumped at the chance to get back together with him. To prove I'm capable of it.

Not anymore.

I start toward the palazzo, taking the main streets and avoiding the byways. On the corner where two narrow canals meet, a few hundred feet before the building, I notice a motorboat in the shadows, moored at one of the small private quays. Parking in Venice is at a premium, and I see the boat is a sleek black model, the kind that well-off families in Venice use to get around, like people in the States have a Cadillac or a Mercedes. Gondolas are a tourist attraction. No one takes a gondola to do errands.

Then I sense movement in the shadows hugging the building by the quay and turn away. I resist a spike of fear. This is what Hugh was worried about. Thieves hiding in the darkness, waiting for a single woman to walk by to steal their pocketbook. Serious crime in Venice is rare, but pickpockets are endemic.

As I turn, I glimpse a swift lunge in my direction, a hand reaching out as if to stop me. A ring flashes gold in the dying light. I slam to a halt. Exactly the wrong thing to do—except something about that ring is oddly familiar.

And then I hear the low laughter, the rumble deep in the chest.

I stare into the gloom as he steps forward.

No. It's not possible.

"Princess. Did I scare you?"

I can't speak, staring at him with my heart in my throat.

"I did. Forgive me. I've been waiting for you. I thought you might spend the night with Hugh after such a lovely afternoon. He always was so...persistent."

"You—you've been watching me?" My voice sounds strangled.

"Watching out for you is more like it."

"Why?"

"Why?" He cocks his head as if he's disappointed. Like he used to do when I showed him an inferior piece of work. That chastising look: *You can do better, Ania.* "Because of this dangerous game you play. With me, of all people. Did you think you could actually win?"

"I have won." I lift my chin. The gall of him.

"Have you?" He smiles. "You're my daughter. But I came first. I can outthink you."

"Don't be so sure."

"Who's being too sure? Aren't you in a bit of trouble? Didn't your plan backfire?"

I step back from him. "What do you want?"

"To finish our game. Like old times. Hide-and-seek, remember? Catch me if you can. I always did end up catching you. You never could hide where I couldn't find you."

"I'm not playing a game." The fury bolts up inside me, a flame igniting my voice. "I am going to take you down for what you did to me."

"Is that so? Well, you left the Leopard's glove at the scene. That was your opening move. The next was mine."

I hear my stifled gasp.

He moves to me. I recoil as he kisses me on the forehead like he did when I was a girl, and then he turns back to the quay and leaps aboard the motorboat. In the light of the streetlamps, his ring gleams as he sets his hand on the wheel.

"The next move is yours. Don't take too long. Gabrielli will arrest someone."

He turns on the ignition and speeds the boat into the dusk, the streetlamps glinting off a glass figurehead on the vessel's bow. I watch as it grows smaller and smaller, vanishing into the canal. Only then do I realize what he's done.

My father's move was to steal the Lemon Twist from me.

And now, it's my move to find it. Before it's too late to save Jerome.

Chapter 11

Jerome

I wake up groggy, my head clogged and heavy like being underwater. I feel lousier than before I conked out. Must be the pill. It packed a wallop. I went right under. Checking my wristwatch, I see it's almost seven o'clock. I slept the entire day. Guess I must have needed it.

Staggering up, I tug on my jeans and sweater to go down to the kitchen. I need something to eat. I've had nothing in my stomach since the fancy canapes last night at the party. Between the champagne hangover, the coffees, and then the pill, I'm running on empty. But my search of the cabinets only uncovers a package of biscotti. Inside the fridge, a carton of cream and some stiff salami slices wrapped in wax paper.

I devour them and wash it down with a glass of tap water that tastes faintly of canal. I don't think you're supposed to drink water here out of the tap.

Moving into the living room, I realize she's not back yet. It's dark outside. What the hell? I stand as if confused. She said she was going to do some shopping. Maybe have lunch with someone who'd been at the party and could tell her something.

Someone. Of course. Who else? He stayed at Julie's side like a heroic knight after her dramatic collapse. He must have overheard what Gabrielli asked her and been questioned himself. And Ania knows him very well, right? And I think I know her.

Dammit, Jerome. You idiot.

When I hear the key in the latch, I bolt into the foyer. She walks in with a bag of—

"Food," she says before I can ask. "I stopped by a local store. Nothing was open but this one shop nearby for tourists. I got us a bottle of wine. Bananas and apples. Prosciutto. Cheese. Bread. Unless you want to go out to a restaurant?"

"No," I mutter. "That sounds great. As long as it's not salami." I can taste it in the back of my throat. I shouldn't have eaten it. Who knows how long it was in the fridge?

"Did you sleep okay?" she asks as I trail after her into the kitchen.

"Like the dead. Are you sure those pills are legal?"

She smiles faintly, taking the stuff from the bag. As she turns to a cabinet to fetch plates and cutlery, I say, "Are you hungry already? I thought you had lunch."

"I did. Hours ago. You didn't. You must be starving."

"Yeah."

She pauses, glancing at me.

"Both," I clarify.

She nods. "I had lunch with Hugh," she says, slicing up the baguette.

"I figured."

"It's not like that."

"Really? From what I saw last night, he seems to think it is."

"Jerome." She unwraps the cheese and the slices of prosciutto. "Please, let's not start this again. He was there. He invited me to dinner or lunch."

"So, it *is* like that. He invited you out. Gotta hand it to the guy. He's got balls. Made his move right in front of me."

She cuts the bananas and apples into a bowl. A fruit salad. I suddenly feel like a jerk. She stopped to buy me food. She thought of me. Of how hungry I would be.

"Hugh was always too sure of himself," she says, but there's a hint of something else in her voice that I can't decipher. "I still got him to tell me what he knew."

"And?"

We start eating at the counter. Or rather, I do. She stands back, watching me before reaching for the wine bottle to uncork it.

"Gabrielli." She wiggles the cork out. "He asked about you."

"He did?" I pause, my mouth full of cheese and bread.

"Yes." She pours me a glass of wine, but before I can take it up to gulp it down, she adds a measure of water from another bottle, diluting it. "I need you sober," she says.

"That bad, huh?"

"I don't know." She doesn't serve herself a glass. She's not eating, either. "He asked if Hugh had met or seen you before last night. If he knew anything about you."

"Like he asked Lauren Segal." I feel queasy.

"We can assume he asked everyone the same thing."

"But why? Why me?" I ask, though I already know. Small circle.

She confirms it. "He's familiar with everyone else. Not on a first-name basis, of course, but all guests of the Contessa Maglione—"

"All rich people, with no reason to steal her necklace."

"Precisely." Her voice is composed. I don't think she feels calm, but she's in absolute control of whatever she *is* feeling. The businesswoman I met in Cannes. Even with her entire collection stolen, she remained in perfect control of herself. I admired it at the time, though it also unnerved me. It still does.

"And something else," she says.

I take the bottle and pour myself a full glass. No water. Screw it.

"Gabrielli spoke again to Julie after we left. Hugh overheard them. He asked her approximately what time she went upstairs to leave the necklace. He mentioned the bodyguard."

"Boulder," I say. When she frowns, I explain, "That big guy in the suit who was right behind her when she came charging in for her camera-ready scene."

She nods. "I'd seem him already. Before."

"You did?"

"Yes. He came upstairs when I was about to enter the wrong room. There were more doors than on the floorplan. He didn't see me, but it was…close. He stayed on the landing, looking down into the foyer. As if he—"

"Was searching for something," I cut in. "Someone."

"That's what I thought. But whatever he thought he saw, he didn't search the bedrooms. Obviously. And when I went back downstairs, he was gone."

"A ghost." Suddenly, I can't drink the wine. "I never spotted him, either. I looked for any signs of surveillance. I was careful. The guy's a professional. He knew to keep out of sight."

"Gabrielli told Julie that the bodyguard thought he saw someone sneak upstairs. But Hugh thinks the situation wasn't all that clear to Gabrielli. Julie couldn't recall exactly what time she left the necklace, other than before the dancing started. And no one, including Hugh, remembers seeing the bodyguard in the ballroom."

"Our alibi. Not so airtight now."

"Depends. If the bodyguard never went into the ballroom, maybe he can't say when Julie started dancing with you. And if he can't confirm that he actually saw anyone go upstairs, and the only person who admits being upstairs is Julie, maybe Gabrielli is confused."

"That's a lot of maybes, isn't it?"

"It's what we have."

"And no passport."

"Yes. About that." She takes a breath. "As far as I can tell, Gabrielli hasn't questioned anyone else again. He didn't sleep last night, either. He might make the rounds later. But Hugh was surprised when I suggested it."

"I'll bet. He probably hasn't had a thing confiscated from him in his entire life."

Her smile is thin. "Jerome, he wanted to help. He's concerned for me. A necklace made by my father, stolen by the Leopard—"

"Wait. He said that? That the Leopard stole it? He used those exact words?"

She takes a small step back, leaning against the counter. "The glove. Everyone saw Julie drop it. The bodyguard gave it to the police. No one's saying it aloud, but..."

"It's implied. Like you wanted it to be." I bite into my bread, but I'm not hungry anymore. It tastes like ash. "And if the Leopard did it, it couldn't be one of the rich people with no reason to steal it. It has to be someone else. The stranger in their midst."

She goes quiet for a moment, a pained look on her face—her first visible sign of discomfort. Though nothing of what she's told me makes me feel any better, that slight wince of hers does. At least, she cares about what happens to me.

"Gabrielli might think so. Under the circumstances, he'll want a quick solution. Julie is making noises about going to the newspapers. Hugh says she threatened to call a press conference, like it's a movie premiere. Gabrielli had to warn her that if she speaks to reporters, it'll complicate the case. But someone already has. An item in the *L.A Daily* this morning. A society columnist called Tattle-Dove. Anonymous, no one knows who it is, but whoever it is was at the party. Or knows someone who was. They cited the glove, said the Leopard had struck again. Here in Venice."

"Christ." I prop my elbows on the counter. I feel as if I might actually vomit.

"It's just a silly gossip column. But it's public now."

"And your father will read it. He'll know. Mission accomplished."

She suddenly moves past me. I follow her into the living room.

"I'm sorry," she whispers, so quietly that I almost don't hear it. "You were right. I should have told you about the glove. I thought—"

"Yeah." I try to sound accepting of her apology. "I know. Bait the trap. Lure him out."

"Yes."

"We're in deep shit, Ania."

She swallows and turns to the window—the view.

"What are we going to do? I can't leave. The necklace is missing. He has my passport. Maybe you should pack up and go before he gets too close."

"Who?" I hear a shiver in her voice.

"Gabrielli. Who else? He's going to come after me. I'll bet my passport on it."

"No." She turns back to me. "He has no proof. Just suspicion. Gossip and innuendo. I'm not leaving you alone to deal with this. Do you think I'm capable of that?"

I lower my eyes. "Of course, not. I just thought—"

She steps closer. I feel her hand on my jaw. "You need a shave," she says. And then, soft but resolute as if it's not up for debate, adds, "I am *not* leaving you."

I pull her to me. So slight. A whisper of a woman. Barely there. But her mouth is warm. Insistent. Her hands under my sweater, roving. Touching. Demanding.

"Let's not think about it tonight," she breathes. "Just for tonight."

That's fine with me. I can't think anymore. I just want to lose myself in her, in the smell and taste of her skin.

And forget I'm being targeted for a crime that I helped to commit.

Afterwards, as she lays in my arms, fast asleep, her hair swept across my chest, I stay awake. I'm not tired. Only sore from our exertions, her fervor surprising me, as if we hadn't made love in weeks and might never do it again.

But now that we've spent ourselves, I return to the thing we can't avoid.

Gabrielli hasn't questioned anyone else since last night. It could be as she said. He hadn't slept, so after due diligence, he's catching some well-deserved shut-eye. Or he's biding his time. To let interrupted lives resume, the theft relegated to a gossip column and whispered asides over luncheons. To wait for their stories to get muddled by shared confidences. To make the mistake he needs.

Or he already knows. He has his suspect. The passport. Now, it's a matter of putting the events at the party together and gathering the necessary evidence to make his arrest.

Still, Ania is right. He has no proof. No evidence. No necklace. It's all circumstantial. Italy isn't America, though. I saw enough during the war to know that justice rarely prevails. Even so, you can't arrest someone without evidence. Just because I'm a stranger doesn't mean I'm a thief, not under the law. He could detain me anyway. But will his case hold up? And how will I defend myself? Ania has plenty of money to hire an attorney, but a foreigner accused of a crime abroad—it might not be so easy to defend. It might take time.

Time I'll spend locked up in a Venetian jail.

And I can't let Ania be involved if I'm arrested. She stole the necklace. If we don't find it—and chances are looking like we won't—whoever took it knows we did it. They knew where to steal it and might show up at any moment to blackmail us. Her money could be our undoing. If the necklace isn't returned to the police, the only other logical reason for taking it would be money. They'll try to force us to pay for their silence. And that never ends well. Once the blackmail starts, it inevitably goes downhill.

She has to be somewhere they can't get to her. They'll have the necklace but no one to threaten if she's gone and I'm behind bars. Then the joke's on them.

I'd almost laugh if it was funny. The thieves who stole from the thieves will be left holding the bag. But it's not funny. My ass is on the line.

I have to do something. Find another alibi, someone who can vouch that I was visible downstairs all night. It can't be Ania. I was her date. She needs to remain clear of it.

Who?

And then it occurs to me. Lauren Segal. She saw me on the dance floor. She winked at me. She spoke to me about an hour or so before. I don't know her well, but she said in the café that she liked me. It's worth a shot. I'm not asking her to lie. Just to come forward if needed to say that she saw me at a certain place at a certain time. That's all it takes, right? Reasonable doubt. You have to be guilty beyond doubt before they can convict you. Even in Italy.

It's not much to go on. But it's all I have.

I need another alibi. Fast.

The staff is there when I wake from a shallow sleep. I hear the housekeeper talking to Ania in Italian. She's already up, dressed, and at the living room table. A buffet platter of scrambled eggs, fruit, bread, and bacon awaits. The smell of fresh coffee beckons.

"Nice spread," I say, taking my seat.

She has her glasses on, picking at her fruit as she reviews a folder. "I need to call the office," she says, glancing at me as I dig into the food. "Before it's too late there. Okay?"

"Sure." I nod. "I need to go out anyway, buy some cigarettes. I'm out."

"You could quit."

"You really never have smoked, have you? No idea."

"My mother smoked, remember?"

"Yeah, well, I'm not dying today of smoking." As soon as I speak, I regret it. Her face tightens. Crappy and insensitive thing to say. "Sorry, that was stupid of me."

She returns her focus to her papers. "Don't be gone long. We need to figure out what to do next. My calls shouldn't take more than an hour or so."

"Right." I finish my breakfast and stand, stretching, my belly full. "Quick shave and shower. Say hi to Mr. Cologne for me."

"Luke," she says tersely as I leave. "His name is Luke. Honestly, Jerome."

She's on the phone when I depart the palazzo. The housekeeper is running a vacuum cleaner in the foyer. As usual, I have to stop to regain my bearings, thinking of the easiest way to San Marco. My walk last night was a series of fortunate accidents. I stumbled upon the main piazza by luck. With the sun out and the sound of water lapping against stone, I wonder if I'll be lucky again or end up trapped in this labyrinth.

At a corner kiosk, I buy cigarettes and an overpriced city map. Consult it. Then weave my way through the corkscrew of streets to the main hotel area. The Danieli is listed on the map. So is the opera house La Fenice and other important sites of interest.

The hotel is stately. Shouts, *"You can't afford me."* The lobby is wallpapered in creamy damask. Enormous chandeliers. Gilt-framed portraits and blackamoor statues. The nine yards of old-world elegance. At the desk, I ask the concierge to call Lauren Segal's room. Give my name. He pauses as if debating my request, then sniffs and does it.

"Signorina Segal will be down in fifteen minutes," he informs me. "You can wait in the restaurant if you like. We're still serving breakfast."

"No, here's fine. Thanks." I linger awkwardly in the lobby, the sofas and chairs looking too pristine to use, like props on a palatial set. People walk around me, eager tourists heading out to see the sights. An impossibly slim older woman in sunglasses with a poodle on a leash. An older couple dressed as if for a cruise. Rich people.

"Oh, hey!" Lauren bounds up to me, wearing the same slacks and red flannel jacket as before, which I unexpectedly appreciate. No pretension. Not dolled-up. What you see is what you get.

"Surprised?"

"I'll say. I didn't—" She shrugs. "Never mind. Got a cigarette? I'm dying for one."

I chuckle. "Sure."

"Not in here." She leads me out to the square. Pigeons scatter. The domes of the Basilica gleam. "How are you liking it so far?"

I light two cigarettes and hand one to her. "It's okay."

"Okay?" She inhales, blows out smoke. "You don't sound okay."

"Yeah." I move to a nearby café. We take a seat outside with a view of the square. Order espresso. She doesn't press me, seems content to sit and smoke, taking in the splendor. The fairy tale her Daddy can afford.

Always gets his money's worth.

"Look." I clear my throat. "I don't want to be pushy."

"Oh, please." She laughs. That warm, spontaneous laugh. "I like pushy. I'm used to it. I'm from Hollywood. Everyone's pushy there."

I have to smile. "You like it?"

"It's what I know. What's not to like?"

Friendly as California.

"You see, I might need a favor," I say and hear the awkwardness in my tone. Light another cigarette as if smoking can disguise it.

She sips her espresso, taking it like I do: two cubes of sugar. She waits.

"I'm in a bit of a jam," I go on, thinking this wasn't such a good idea. Her eyes are a startling clear green like an ocean when the light hits it. Lovely eyes. Interested but not inquisitive. Not pushy.

"I'm listening," she eventually says when I don't continue.

"That inspector…he—" I resist the urge to look around as if Gabrielli might be lurking under the awning. It's so ridiculous.

"Has you in his sights?" she says as if reading my mind. My very words to Ania.

"How did you know?"

"Not like it's top-secret." She laughs again, but less warm now. A touch of seriousness. "He asked about you at the party. Must have asked everyone, I assume."

"Assume?"

"Well. He did ask me. And my father. Did he ask your spectacular friend?"

"Ania?" Just saying her name aloud sounds like a betrayal.

"Yes. Her."

"Not much at first. But he came to see us yesterday. He asked more then."

"Huh." She helps herself to my cigarette pack. "Like I said, not top-secret. How'd she take it? She doesn't seem like the type you can drop in on unannounced."

"You don't like her very much, do you?" I remark.

"Me?" She hesitates. "I don't know her. No one does. I mean, she's famous and all that. Virgil Thorne's daughter. Jeweler to the stars. But no one really knows her."

"I do," I say quietly.

She looks down. "I guessed as much."

"Lauren." At my voicing of her name, she lifts her face. I see it, then. Yeah. She does like me. She's attracted to me. It's been a long time since I've seen that particular look in a woman's eyes but I've not forgotten it. Ania never has that look. I can tell when she's admiring me, my physique. I know when she's interested. But this covert look, the way a woman tilts her face just so as if gauging her chances...it's not an Ania look. Ania never has to gauge her chances. She already knows what her chances are.

"He took my passport." I didn't plan on saying it, not so soon—or ever.

Her eyes widen a fraction. "Wow. He really does have you in his sights." The way she declares it turns my blood cold. Gabrielli hasn't questioned anyone else again. Hasn't confiscated other passports or made his rounds. Probably doesn't have any plans to.

"You think?" I manage to say.

"Yeah." She taps ash on the saucer. "Small circle, as I said. It can't possibly be one of them. Who would dare?" She leans to me, lowering her voice. Conspiratorial again. The outsiders sharing a secret like at the party. "Between you and me, I think plenty of them would dare if they could. Vintage Thorne. A rare diamond. Who wouldn't want it?"

"To wear," I counter. "To show off. You can't show off a stolen diamond."

"Right." She sits back. "So, they wouldn't dare. No point."

"But me? I would?"

"Did I say that? I said it's a small circle. They all envy each other—"

"Not Ania."

She pauses. "Well. With looks like hers and all her money, why should she?"

I nod, acutely uncomfortable now. As if I'm planning to commit another crime.

"They're not nice people," she goes on. "You're not part of their circle. So, if the inspector asks, they point in the direction he's headed. It's what they do."

"But not you."

"No." Now, she appears uncomfortable. "I told him the truth."

I let the silence lengthen between us. This is my opening. Do I risk it?

"If he comes after me..." I finally say.

"Yes?" She waits again.

"I might need an alibi."

She sits quietly for a long moment. But I can sense the gears churning behind her silence. She's not stupid. She's the daughter of a Hollywood mogul. Not pushy. But no fool.

"I told him the truth," she says again.

"I was dancing with Julie when the necklace was stolen," I venture as if walking across fractured ice. "You saw me."

"Did I?" She pauses, her nose scrunching up. "Oh, right. I did. God, she had you in her claws, didn't she? Not nice people. She's one of the worst. Couldn't make it to the top of the heap in pictures, so she went and married a rich old guy who thinks she's the queen of Sheba. Now, she acts like she was a star. She wasn't. Her pictures lost money. My father would have voided her contract if she hadn't gone off to play contessa."

Daughter of a Hollywood mogul. Knows her way around a box-office profit sheet.

"But you saw me," I say, returning to my point. "I was there. Not upstairs."

She nods. "I remember. And then you went to talk to Ania Thorne."

"And before, we talked, too."

"We did." A flush of color in her freckled cheeks. "I was pushy, then. Huh?"

"No. I liked that you were nice to me. No one else was."

"They're not nice to me, either." She turns her head to gaze at the square. There's something harsh in her voice. Resentment. "Picture people. Not East Coast. Not upper-crust. They'll gladly eat Julie's caviar and drink her champagne. Not ours."

"She used to be in pictures," I say. "Doesn't that count? She's not upper-crust."

"But a countess, wouldn't you know? A palazzo. C'mon. Small circle."

"I'm beginning to see that." I light my third cigarette and drain my espresso to the dregs.

"I'll do it," she says abruptly. She stares into my eyes. What you see is what you get. "Your alibi. If he comes after you. You didn't steal the necklace. Did you?"

I suddenly hear myself laugh. "No."

"I didn't think so. And there's the glove."

I tense. "The glove."

"Yes. The glove. No one's saying it—well, not in public anyway. The inspector made quite the show of insisting we keep our mouths shut. No one will. How can they? The Leopard crashed our party. It's the most excitement they've had in years. Better than Julie's caviar. And to see her in such a state—"

"Not nice people," I say.

She nods. "Now, no one can show off the rare diamond."

"Do you really think...?"

A shrug. "Who knows? The glove is his mark. His spoor. I was here, and now your necklace isn't. It's a great story if nothing else."

"For the movies."

"Exactly. My dad is already planning a script for Audrey Hepburn." She smiles. "Not upper-crust. We make our money the old-fashioned way. We work for it."

"I really appreciate it." I feel as if I can't get off the chair. Like everything inside me has drained into a puddle at my feet.

"Hey. Not upper-crust means we have to look out for each other." She gestures to the waiter for the check.

I feel bad. As if I've used her. "We could—I don't know. Visit a museum or something."

"A museum?" She grimaces. "I've had it up to here with churches and museums. Take me dancing instead. Or to a movie."

I open my wallet to pay the tab. "Do they have movie theaters in Venice?"

"My father would never come here if they didn't. Gondola drive-ins."

"Really?"

She bursts out laughing. "Wouldn't that be something? With soggy popcorn."

We walk back to the hotel. In the lobby, I pause. Reach out my hand. "I really do appreciate it."

"You already said that." She gets on her tiptoes and kisses my cheek. "Don't be a stranger," she whispers.

And then she bounds up the staircase.

I turn, thinking I should be relieved. She's reliable. Not stupid. I can count on her.

But whatever relief I feel is shattered when I see a man rise from one of those impressive throne-like chairs by the far wall.

Gabrielli.

Chapter 12

Ania

I wait until I hear Jerome leave, then quickly finish my call to the Los Angeles office and dial the operator to connect me to our New York office. Luke is there at the moment, my second-in-charge. He travels between L.A. and New York as co-director, much like I did, to ensure that the coastal branches of Thorne & Company are coordinated. But our Los Angeles branch is glitzier, catering to the stars, and Luke is a stalwart New Yorker. The brazen sunshine and sycophancy of Hollywood, he says, offends his repressed East Coast sensibilities—one of the traits he has in common with my father.

His phone rings several times. I check my wristwatch. I'm six hours ahead of him; it's four o'clock in the afternoon in New York, but he might have left the office early to beat the traffic. Still, his secretary should be picking up.

Then I hear his voice: "Yes? Hello? Luke Westerly."

"Luke." I can't disguise the relief in my voice. "You're there."

"Why, yes, my sweet. Where else would I be? I'm a slave to Thorne & Company."

I laugh. "As bad as that?"

"Not really. But it sounds very dramatic, doesn't it?" He chuckles. I can see him at his desk, in his tailored Saville Row suit—only the finest for Luke—his handsome, gym-toned form groomed to perfection, his handkerchief matching the color of his tie, his jacket unbuttoned to display his close-fitting patterned vest with a touch of flair.

"And I must tell you, Ania, that while your leave of absence is no doubt well-deserved, and I'm very appreciative of my promotion, my love life is in ruins. I found myself eyeing my waiter at lunch today. My *waiter*. I trust yours is better? The rugged Mr. Curtis still loyal at your side? One of us has to be having some fun, after all."

"Oh, Luke." I sigh. "I miss you."

"And I miss you, Ania. It's not the same without you, though I rather enjoy marching about like Caligula, issuing imperial mandates."

"The board's not giving you any grief?" I ask.

"Not at all. They seem rather pleased, actually." He lowers his voice, teasing me. "A man in charge. It always makes them less anxious. That, and of course, the quarterly profit reports. As long as they see the green, well—what is there to complain about?"

I laugh again. I can't remember the last time I laughed. Luke is more than just a trusted business colleague to me. He's like my favorite uncle, my older brother, my best friend, and confidant all rolled into an irresistible package. If he weren't inclined to bat for his own team, we've always joked that we'd make the perfect couple. My father thought so, too. He encouraged it, in fact, until Luke felt obliged to inform him that he could never see me that way, even if he didn't have a fatal weakness for matadors. Papa was horrified. He never brought it up again. "Luke, I...I need your advice."

"Based on what I read today in that dreadful society column, I'm not surprised. I can't believe you were even at that party. Well, I can believe the party, but not the robbery. It must have happened under your nose. Just like Cannes. Ania, my sweet, you have an astonishing knack for putting yourself in the most awkward situations."

It was nothing like Cannes, I think, but of course I don't say it.

"It's worse than Cannes, Luke."

"How? It wasn't your collection. Though, yes, one of our pieces."

I don't realize I've gone quiet until he says, "Ania, what is it? Don't get me wrong, I love that you turn to me when you're in one of these awkward situations, but the papers haven't reported that anyone was harmed. I can imagine the uproar. Julie Kimbell. She must have created such a stink. But you're all right? You didn't go and try to stop the thief, I hope. After our fiasco in Paris, we must never attempt that again, exciting as it was."

"No, I'm not hurt. It's just… I don't know who to trust right now."

He goes silent for a moment. "Not even the rugged Mr. Curtis?"

"No. I mean, yes. I trust Jerome, of course. But, Luke… He's become the prime suspect. The police confiscated his passport. "

"Really? Why on earth would they suspect him? He's as upstanding as the Statue of Liberty. And nearly as tall."

"He's a stranger. You know how it is. Everyone at the party. Julie's friends."

"Julie has friends now? How alarming."

I have to smile. "Acquaintances. But still."

"Yes. I do know how it is," he says. "Unfortunately for our Mr. Curtis. But while he may be an outsider to the society relics, he's still with you. What would be his motive? And I can't imagine they have any evidence."

"None. But I'm afraid that won't clear him. It was Julie's annual gala. Over a hundred people, with everyone singing the same tune. No one knows exactly what time the necklace was taken, so no one knows where anyone was at any given moment."

"That's absurd. Jerome? He's a war hero, for goodness' sake. What would he want with that necklace? The clasp is defective," he adds, sniffing. A company man to his bones.

"Nothing," I say. I feel awful. I hate lying to Luke. I've wanted to tell him for months what I discovered about my father, but it would put him in an untenable position. He worked under Virgil Thorne for years. Admired and respected him. And now, he's my co-director, my link to the company I can't lose control of. If he knows what I'm doing, and why I'm doing it, it'll force him to either be my accomplice or compel him to report it to the board. Either way, it won't be pleasant for the business or either of us.

"I know Jerome is innocent," I say.

"Of course, he is. Tell the police that."

If only I could. Am I so selfish that I won't turn myself in, if it comes down to Jerome or me? I suppose I would, but that won't exculpate him. He's staying with me. He was my date at the party. They'll never believe I could have done it without his knowledge. We'll both end up in jail. Besides, I know who took the necklace and who has it. I just need to figure out where my father is. But I'm so nervous; I'm having a hard time thinking straight.

"It would be my word about my friend," I say. "How credible is that? Luke, I have to get Jerome out of this mess."

"I completely understand. I wish I could fly over and whisk you both away."

"I wish you could, too."

"Well, I'm here. You can trust me. And trust Jerome. I wouldn't trust anyone else *but* him under the circumstances. The man is gold, Ania. Unpolished, but gold all the same."

I draw in a steadying breath. "Luke, my father trusted you, too, didn't he?"

"Your father? Why, yes. But what does Virgil have to do with any of this?"

I hope I haven't gone too far. Luke was the one who saw my father's signature ring during the car accident in Paris; he won't ever bring it up to me, not unless I mention it first, but that's enough damning evidence for him to suspect my father. I can't add to any suspicions Luke might already have; knowing his loyalty to my father, he's most likely decided to brush the ring aside as strange coincidence. But I also need more information. I have to retrieve the necklace and see it returned to Julie. It's the only way to protect Jerome.

"You were his right-hand. Like you are for me. You saw everything. What was he like during those weeks before the board ousted him?"

Luke pauses as if my question caught him by surprise. Then he laughs. "You know as well as anyone; your father never liked to show his emotions. Always calm, cool, and collected. Like you. He kept insisting the lawsuits were nonsense. That he'd win every one. That he had it under control."

"Yes, but how was he planning to do it?"

"He kept that to himself, along with whatever else he was feeling."

"But didn't he feel responsible for the financial losses? For our reputation?"

"I imagine so." Luke pauses again. "As I recall, he did mention a plan around that time. I remember thinking it was rather unusual but brilliant, like most of his ideas. He hoped it would solve everything. You know how much he loved New York and never wanted to live anywhere else? Well, in those last weeks, he asked me to look into him possibly moving to Venice. To your godmother's palazzo, to start up a new business venture with his friend, Gianni Volpato."

"Who owns the glass factory here," I say. "I apprenticed with Gianni."

"I remember. Your father did, too. He recalled how well that limited line you made sold for us and proposed a new unique glass jewelry collection. Like Lalique, he said, who'd been a jeweler at first and moved on to work exclusively in glass, making a fortune. Virgil had me consult our lawyers about extradition or lawsuits following him to Italy."

"So, he *was* worried. What happened?"

"Well. Legally, moving abroad wouldn't have resolved anything. He was still the company director and liable. And several of those lawsuits, as you know, were filed against him for personal damages, so he couldn't slip out of the country and hope they'd go away. As for his plans for the glass line, as far as I know, he was very keen on it, believed it would bring profit and stifle the rumors of his imminent beheading by the board."

"But he never made the line?"

"No. He was ousted too soon. He did sketch a few designs. Do you want me to search our files? He must have left them here. In the ensuing chaos after the board removed him, he was treated appallingly. Escorted off the premises by a security team hired by the board. Not allowed to take any company property with him." Luke makes a disgusted sound. "He didn't deserve it, though those lawsuits were a calamity for us. Millions to settle them."

"Yes," I say to justify my call. "Please, if you can search the files, I'd appreciate it. Thank you, Luke. For everything."

"Ania," he says. "Have you spoken to him?"

"To...my father?"

"Yes. No one seems to know where he is. I telephoned Gerard at the penthouse. I wanted to invite Virgil to dinner, maybe an opera at the Met. I thought he must be lonely, shut up there all alone while you gallivant about Europe with your lover. But Gerard told me he'd left New York and hasn't communicated his whereabouts."

"No," I reply quietly. "He hasn't contacted me, either."

"How odd. Virgil was always prone to solitude, like most creative people. But months of incommunicado? It's not like him."

"I'm sure he's fine. I'll check in at the villa on Lake Garda. And London, once the situation here is resolved. He could be with Michael and Agnes. He's retired now, and not by choice. He probably wants to travel and be incommunicado for a while."

"Well, do let me know if you reach him. Tell him when he returns to New York, I want to take him out to dinner."

"Yes, I will, Luke. Goodbye for now."

"*Ciao*, Ania. And my sweet, do give that devastating man of yours a hug from me. Tell him, Mr. Cologne remembers him fondly and still knows how to shoot a gun."

I let out a halting laugh as we hang up.

My mind is reeling. I ask the housekeeper Lucia for another cup of espresso and check my watch. It's been nearly two hours. Where is Jerome? I don't like him being out there alone on the streets.

Months of incommunicado? It's not like him.

If Luke only knew.

I pace to the window. A motorboat whisks by, splicing the waters.

A boat...

It suddenly hits me what it was about that boat my father sped away in last night. The ornament on the bow. It wasn't a typical Venetian crest. Instead, it was made of golden-colored glass that shone in the lamplight. A crest used by only one family in Venice, designed by them over two hundred years ago, handblown in their factory. That boat belonged to my first boss, one of my father's closest friends, Gianni Volpato. Gianni is retired now, turned over his glass factory, one of Venice's most prestigious, to his son, Paolo, who's about my age.

Of course, my father would stay with him. He couldn't risk a hotel or a rented palazzo; that would make it too easy to track him down. But would Gianni take him in? Why not? He doesn't know my father is a notorious jewel thief.

If my father was on the Volpato boat, then he's on the mainland at their villa. Did they have something to do with my father's plan to steal back the Lemon Twist? No, that wouldn't make sense. Gianni wouldn't have anything to do with theft. My father is probably just using his friend's villa as a safe haven. A place to hide while he plays out his game with me. His sick game of catch-me-if-you-can. Prove who's better.

The door chime startles me. I actually feel the leap under my skin. Who is it? Jerome wouldn't ring. He has a key. Suppliers would come to the back entrance. This is the front door. There's only one person I can think of who'd ring the bell.

Gabrielli.

Has he come to arrest Jerome?

I find myself holding my breath. Listen to Lucia as she opens the door.

A man says in Italian, "A gift for Signorina Thorne."

Not Gabrielli. Lucia chides the delivery man for using the front door.

I try to contain my anxiety as she comes into the living room and hands me a box wrapped in red and silver paper with an elaborate silver bow.

I look at the silver medallion in the middle. The name of the store: *Volpato Artistica*.

This can't be a coincidence.

My hands tremble as I unravel the ribbon and let it fall to the floor. A silver snake unfurling, coiling at my feet as I pull off the paper and open the white box.

Inside, a beautiful Murano figurine.

A miniature glass leopard.

Chapter 13

Jerome

I stand still for a second, then make myself walk toward him. No use in pretending I haven't seen him. He's looking right at me.

Here. In the Danieli. Is he tracking me down? Or is it merely a coincidence? Maybe he's making those rounds I thought he wouldn't, after all.

"Signor Curtis." He's all neat and tidy. Fresh suit. His sparse hair flat on his shiny scalp. A nick on his chin from his morning shave. A masculine scent, though not expensive. Italian cologne, probably available at any corner shop. Forest-smelling, like something I'd use.

"We seem to keep running into each other," I say, shaking his hand and wincing inwardly as I hear the false comradery in my tone.

"Do we?" He smiles. "I'm here on duty. But here you are, as well."

Did he see me with Lauren? He must have. Shit.

"Yes. Here I am," I say lamely.

"I thought you were staying at Signorina Thorne's palazzo."

"I am. I went out for a walk. She's making some business calls." I sound too hasty, too quick to justify myself. I don't owe this guy an explanation. Slow down. The worst he can think is that I've been flirting with the pretty redhead. Well, not the worst, but I still have every right to be here. It's a hotel.

"Ah. Business. Necessary. But boring for you, yes?" He has a briefcase in hand. He switches it to his other hand. "A cigarette outside, perhaps?"

What is it with people who smoke but don't ever buy their own cigarettes?

I nod. "Of course."

We walk outside to the square and light up. He inhales with gusto. "Ah. Very nice. Lovely day, is it not? Not too cold. No rain. A perfect winter's day in Venezia. You are lucky. January is not usually so accommodating."

More chitchat about the weather. Can I finish the cigarette and leave? He doesn't seem to be looking for me. Must be making his rounds. Which is good news. Maybe I'm off the hook. Or if not off, at least one of several worms on his line. Not the only one.

"You see many places here?" he asks. The tourist guide, again.

"Not really. Ania's been busy. And well...the party. The late night. I'm just getting started, to be honest."

"You must. You cannot leave Venezia without seeing her beauty. People pay a lot of money to come here." Is he implying that I haven't? That I'm free-wheeling it on Ania's money? Does he think I'm—what's the Italian word for it— a gigolo?

"I'm sure I will," I say.

"You were in Italy before, yes? During the war?"

"Yes." I stub out my cigarette on the cobblestone. "In Rome. Then Florence."

"Not the same as now."

"Nothing was."

"That is true." A sigh. Sentimental. "So many mistakes made during the war. Mussolini. The *partisanos*. The Germans. Everyone killing each other."

"Don't forget the Jews." I glance at him. "Everyone was killing them."

He goes quiet. Then he nods. "Yes."

Anti-Semitic? It wouldn't surprise me. It's been less than twenty years since the war ended, but the hatred of Jews in Europe is centuries old. It doesn't go away because the Germans went on a mass-murdering rampage. It's still here, just pushed deeper under the surface. Not fashionable to hate Jews in the open anymore. In France, it's illegal. They take their collaboration guilt very seriously. As they should.

"You helped liberate Italy?" he says.

"No. I mean, not really." I hesitate. "It was mostly liberated by the time I got here. I was part of the Allied forces," I go on because he seems to expect it. "But the majority of my service was after the war. In Germany."

"Ah. You mentioned Berlin. Unpleasant, I think."

I don't answer. Berlin after the war couldn't be anything else.

"You may wonder why I ask." He also puts out his cigarette on the cobblestones but then he picks up the butt to deposit it in a nearby trash can. Venezia's beauty. Mustn't dirty it with our filthy habits.

"You see," he goes on, "I ask because I made—how do you say? Inquiries?"

"You did?" Of course, he did. Making his rounds.

"I apologize. Unfortunate. But my duty. So…"

"Necessary." I offer him another cigarette.

He shakes his head. "No, no. Only one. If not, that's how it starts."

"Right." I want to ask where he made his necessary inquiries, but I have the feeling he's going to tell me anyway.

"You were honorably discharged. A patriot."

"I was just doing my job."

"Yes. But in Germany. After the war."

"Lots of other guys like me were doing their jobs in Germany after the war."

"Of course." He takes a moment. "Then you moved to London. You don't go back home. May I ask why?"

I'm taken aback. He made inquiries all right. "I like Europe. I don't have any family left in the States. I figured, why not stay? I chose London because they speak English. With a funny accent, but still."

My feeble attempt at a joke seems to please him. He smiles again. "As an insurance investigator? With Lambert Securities."

"That's right."

"Because of what you did in Germany after the war?"

I suddenly sense danger. "Partly."

"You don't want to speak of it."

"I can't." I make a gesture of regret. "Classified. What I did in Germany."

"Ah." As if he understands. Does he?

"Look, I'm not sure why you're asking me this."

"Oh, curiosity. Italians, we are…*come il gatto*. Curious. You don't mind?"

"I suppose not."

He nods. Takes his time as if we're having a normal conversation. Two men of the world, getting to know each other. "And you met Signorina Thorne in Cannes. She was on business there. You, as well?"

And here it is.

"Yes." I can't lie to him. If he contacted Lambert as part of his official inquiry, they would oblige. They shouldn't because I am—or *was*—an employee, a U.S. citizen, and they need authorization to release my records. But if he cited a crime, a jewelry theft, they'd oblige. They're not happy with me. Not after the way I left them. "She had some jewelry stolen in Cannes. Lambert sent me to investigate."

"And did you?"

What kind of question is that?

"Yes. It was my job."

"And what did you find?"

I clear my throat.

"You can't talk of it," he says. "Classified?"

I nod. "It's her company. Her claim with Lambert. I did my investigation and filed the report." A cursory report, enough to satisfy requirements on an over two-million-dollar claim. Sparse on details. Like I said, they're not happy with me.

"Do you think it was the Leopard?" he asks suddenly.

"The Leopard?"

"Yes. We found a glove at the party. The contessa says it was left on her dressing table where the necklace was. That is something the Leopard does, yes?"

Is he asking me for advice on the case? Have I gone from suspect to colleague?

"I wouldn't know. I'm not that familiar with him."

"You think it's a him?"

I shrug. "Maybe not. Seems likely, though."

"But women. Their passion for jewelry. Why not a woman instead of a man? You don't think they're capable of it?"

"I never said that." Danger. Right under my feet. A chasm. Does he think he has the right man, or is he looking for the right woman?

"No?"

"No. I think women are capable of it." I recall the camps. Ravensbrück. Auschwitz. Bergen-Belsen. The female guards herding Jews into the gas chambers as efficiently as the male ones. No difference as far as remorse went. No contrition.

"But not the Leopard?"

"As I said, I'm not familiar with his case history."

And then I see the trap. Too late. Because he motions to the briefcase. "No? Lambert told me you were very interested. They said you were—obsessed? Is that the word?"

I'm in the chasm.

"I was interested," I say cautiously. "I'm an insurance investigator. It's my job to be interested in a thief who's never been caught. In my spare time, I checked unsolved files that could be connected to him, filed by Lambert. I wasn't obsessed. I was doing my job."

"But you say you're not familiar with his history?"

"Lambert only had one or two files that matched his methods, not his entire history."

"Ah."

Out of the chasm or digging myself in deeper?

"You're no longer an insurance investigator," he says.

"No. I left."

"After Cannes."

"Yes."

"When you met Signorina Thorne?"

What does he really want to know? All of a sudden, I don't care. This dancing around the maypole is getting on my nerves.

"Inspector, am I under suspicion?" I ask bluntly.

"No." He steps back. Our civilized conversation broken by my blunt American candor. "I'm asking. Did you leave your job after meeting Signorina Thorne?"

"I did. She lives in the United States. And Paris. Not London."

"So, you went back home for her. Is it love?"

"Is that your business?"

He makes a sad moue. "I've offended you."

"No. Really, I want to know. How is it your business? People fall in love, don't they? They change jobs. It happens."

"Yes. But you did not change jobs. You left your employer in London. Lambert was angry because, as they told me, you did not do your job in Cannes for them."

Italian candor now. Straight to the gut.

"I did my job. They might not like it because the jewelry was never recovered and they had to settle a large claim, but I did what was required. I filed the report."

"Yes. They told me."

What else did they tell him?

"Signor Curtis. Excuse me, I do not mean to offend, but… You go to Cannes to investigate a spectacular theft from Signoria Thorne's company—"

"Spectacular?" I echo. It sounds melodramatic. Even if it was.

"You do not think so? Exclusive jewelry made for famous film stars. Like the contessa's necklace. A famous necklace for a film actress."

Now she acts like she was a star. She wasn't. Her pictures lost money.

"I guess you could say that."

"Yes, I think it is…no accident. But no glove in Cannes. Or none reported."

"Check the French police records. They conducted an investigation, too. I only went to look into a potential insurance claim, to make sure it wasn't client fraud."

"Fraud?" He's surprised. Or pretending to be. "You think Signorina Thorne…?"

"Not me. Lambert. And they didn't think it. It's routine." I take a moment to return his smile. Mine has teeth, but he's asking for it.

"Clients will do this?" he says.

"Sometimes. They fake a burglary for the insurance money. Not often, but it's still standard procedure to investigate the possibility."

"It was not the case in Cannes," he declares as if it's unthinkable.

"No. It was definitely a robbery."

"But never solved." Stated matter-of-factly. His inquiry.

"It wasn't. I did try my best."

"I see." He turns for a moment to the hotel as if he might be late for an important appointment. "Signor Curtis, may I be honest?" He doesn't wait for my permission. "I have—an enigma. A valuable necklace stolen from the contessa. A glove. And you: a man who investigated a similar theft in Cannes nine months ago but never identified the thief or recovered the jewelry. Who left his employment after filing a large claim—"

"On the client's behalf," I cut in. "At her request."

"Yes, of course. Please, permit me. A large claim. No new job. Traveling with the client. Do you see my enigma?"

"Not really."

"Signor Curtis." A disappointed pause. "You know my duty. You did it yourself."

"I wasn't a police inspector."

"Nevertheless. Investigator. *Commissario*." He chortles. "The jobs are very similar. Like the thefts."

He's connecting the Cannes heist to this one. I'd admire his ingenuity if I weren't so focused on not getting buried in the abyss he's digging under my feet. Because he's not wrong. He's much closer than he thinks.

"I think you understand me," he says.

I swallow.

"A man like you. You would know how to do this. The way to avoid mistakes. To make it look as if someone else did it. Like the Leopard, maybe."

"Are you accusing me—?"

"Not accusing. Signor Curtis, I am just asking. You would know, yes? I would know. It's our job. Inspector. Investigator. We know."

"But we don't do it." I'm breathless now, and it shreds my voice. So close. Too close.

"No. We do not." He lets out a sigh. "Forgive me, I must go. Duty." He moves past me. "You will not leave Venice, yes? I have your word?"

"You have my passport," I remind him.

"I do. *Buona giornata*, Signor Curtis. Please, give my regards to Signorina Thorne."

As he returns to the Danieli, briefcase in hand, so neat and tidy, I have the wild urge to follow him, find out who else he's meeting with. But what good will it do except make me look more suspicious? He's made himself clear.

I have the expertise. The opportunity. He doesn't need a motive. For him, the value of the necklace is motive enough. Why do thieves steal? For money they don't have; money *I* certainly don't have. Traveling with the client. No new job. An angry ex-employer in London. Accusations that I failed to do my duty.

All of it, handed to him on a platter.

Wow. He really does have you in his sights.

It's only a matter of time before he decides to stop asking impromptu questions over cigarettes and goes for my jugular.

Time that is fast running out.

Chapter 14

Ania

No matter what I do, I can't distract myself. I put an opera record on the stereo, uncork a bottle of wine, pick up my copy of the bestseller *Peyton Place*, and try to read. But nothing keeps me from returning to the jungle animal on the table, gleaming in the soft light of the chandelier.

Tiny as it is, it frightens me more than I could have imagined. I have the urge to take the damned thing and fling it at the fireplace. Watch it shatter against the marble. The fragments to be swept up and discarded. But I don't. Instead, I run my fingers over the smooth glass contours and try to figure out my father's next move.

One thing is for certain. I can't involve Jerome. He's an innocent bystander, caught up in this because of his charms and my obsession. I have to do whatever I can to help him, no matter what it costs me or how it affects my fractured relationship with my father. As if there is anything left of the relationship. My father stealing the Lemon Twist is the ultimate betrayal in a gambit I've been trying to decipher since he struck against me in Cannes.

"Ania? What's that?"

I turn. I didn't hear him enter—the strains of the opera muffled his footsteps, and now it's too late to hide the incriminating piece of glass.

As I grapple for an explanation, Jerome picks it up. Examines it. I can see by the darkening of his expression that he understands the symbolism. But he isn't sure what it actually means. I'm surprised by how exhausted and drawn his face is. And shocked that it makes him somehow even sexier. And then I'm even more shocked that given everything going on, my libido can still react.

"What is this?" he asks again.

"Exactly what it looks like," I hear myself say.

"Okay. Let me ask a different question. Why are you sitting here listening to very loud Italian music and playing with a glass leopard that wasn't on this table when I left?" A hint of accusation seeps into his tone.

"Speaking of leaving," I reply. "Where did you go?"

"To hell and back."

He moves to the bar, takes a tumbler, and pours himself a few inches of scotch. Drinking in mid-afternoon isn't like him at all. Glass in hand, he returns to where I've taken a seat. I reach for my glass of wine, take a long sip of the heady red vintage. It's not like me to be drinking in the afternoon, either. But, clearly, we both need the reinforcement.

"Who goes first?" I ask.

"Fine. I'll start." In a flat voice, he tells me about his excursion to the Danieli and the unexpected interrogation by Gabrielli. My stomach cramps as I hear what the inspector put him through. Then, all too soon, he says, "Your turn."

"Can I get you some more?" I motion to his tumbler, to buy myself some time.

"Not yet. I'm not giving you a chance to put off what I'm sure is bound to be a doozy. A glass leopard. C'mon, Ania. That's not subtle. What the hell is going on?"

I pause, draw in a shallow breath, and tell him how the statue arrived, an unexpected and wholly unwanted gift.

"It arrived after I left?" he says.

"I wasn't going to tell you. I've been trying to protect you from this. From my mess."

"I don't need you to protect me, Ania. I need you to tell me everything. And I want you to do it now. I mean it."

I've seen him angry before, but not quite like this. His entire person is rigid. It makes me think of how he used to hunt Nazis after the war. I can't blame him for it, even if at the same time, I resent the insinuation that I've been lying to him. Because I have been.

I take another sip of my wine and explain it.

He sits in utter silence, his face unreadable until he says, "Your father is here? In Venice? You spoke to him?"

"He was waiting for me after my visit with Hugh. He appeared out of nowhere. He had a motorboat. I recognized the crest on it."

"Did he threaten you?"

"You could say that." I down the rest of my wine. "He admitted he took the necklace, so I guess we can take that as a threat."

"We should have known. Who else would have managed to get inside the family palazzo?" He lets out a dry chuckle, no humor in it. "God. Some thieves we turned out to be. We completely screwed this up."

"It gets worse." I falter for a moment as the reality threatens to overwhelm me. "This statue. I think it's a message. It has to be. It's made by the Murano glass factory owned by his friend, Gianni Volpato, who also owns the motorboat. I did an apprenticeship at the factory when I was nineteen. My father arranged it for me."

"Murano?" He frowns. "Isn't that a local tourist trap?"

"It's an island to the north. About twenty minutes from here by boat. In the thirteenth century, Murano became the manufacturing center for Venetian glass. I designed a line of glass jewelry during my time there. I called Luke today," I go on. "He mentioned that my father was planning to add a new glass line to our collection just before he was ousted by the board. He thought it would bring in extra profit, stem the crisis from the lawsuits against him. Jerome, those lawsuits were the very reason he was removed as director and banned from the company. Why I was appointed to take his place. None of this can be a coincidence. My glass line was something he planned to replicate to save himself."

"Wait a sec." He holds up his hand. "Your father took the necklace and is inviting you to your old training ground to—what? Have it out with him? I don't get it. What's his game? He's put us in a very tough spot."

"Which I plan to get us out of," I retort, more harshly than intended.

"How?"

"How else? I have to go to Murano. Tonight."

"Tonight?"

"Yes. There are tourists during the day. Workers. No one will be there at night."

"So, now we're breaking into a glass factory?"

"We're not breaking in." I give him an exasperated look. "I spent a year working there. It belongs to a close family friend. I know my way around. Trust me."

"Trusting you is how we got into this jam," he mutters.

But he knows we have no other choice. Because of this inexplicable chemistry between us and because—well, because he has to trust me.

Just as I have to trust him. We have no one else.

"Then I'm going with you," he says.

"That's not necessary. It's too much of a risk," I say at once, for no reason that makes any sense. Except that I don't want him and my father coming face-to-face.

"A risk?" He laughs. "I'm about to be arrested. It doesn't get much riskier than that. I'm not letting you go alone to whatever trap he's preparing for you."

"You...you think it's a trap?"

"Ania." He stares at me. "If Virgil somehow knew we planned to steal that necklace and followed us here on purpose, then took the necklace to dangle it in your face—yeah, I'd say it's a trap. He's up to something. And whatever it is, it can't be good."

I feel so foolish. So naïve. Of course, he's right. My father isn't playing this game for kicks. Not anymore, if he ever did. He has an ulterior motive, and it terrifies me that I can't figure it out. That he's always one step ahead of me.

"Fine. We'll take the vaporetto. But I'm driving."

We spend the next few hours preparing as the sun goes down. Maria serves us a homecooked meal, but Jerome barely touches the food, though he's always had a hearty appetite. Then he goes out to the mooring dock to fuel the boat. I force myself to eat something before I change into warm, dark clothes.

By the time we're motoring north upon the canal, he's brooding, swathed in his peacoat and wool cap, staring into the mist-bound night. The water is choppy, and the fog hides the moon, but the canals are marked by light-posts to steer by, and I've driven this route before. I used to take this same vaporetto every day to Murano, reveling in the novelty of being nineteen, away from my family and on my own for the first time.

It turns out Jerome is more knowledgeable about nautical maneuvering than I thought. He sounds like an experienced sailor as he warns me about the hidden mud silts and other unseen watery pitfalls we have to avoid.

"I really do know my way," I say tersely. "I told you to trust me."

"You know the way there at night?" he retorts.

"Yes. I sometimes left the factory very late and drove myself home at night. Alone." I meet his skeptical stare. "I'm not helpless."

"Right. My mistake." But he can't help himself, and I almost don't mind that during the trip he keeps calling out warnings. I actually start to like it; his incorrigible need to assert control as we near the cemetery island, and I point it out to him.

"San Michele. Where the Venetians come to bury their dead. In the early 1800s, Napoleon invaded Venice and declared it illegal."

"He had a point. Not very hygienic, burying people on an island built on poles," he remarks, reminding me again of what he must have seen during the war.

"There isn't much choice here. Only it became so crowded that now the dead can only be buried for ten to twenty years—or ninety-nine years if it's a family mausoleum."

"Huh. What happens after that?"

"The remains have to be moved to another cemetery. They're usually cremated," I say and then wince. Cremation must bring up unpleasant memories for him, too.

He goes silent as I propel the boat past San Michele toward our destination.

I throttle the engine as we drift into the side canal that leads to the back entrance of the factory. Peering around, I search for other vessels, where the workers and Gianni usually dock. All the reserved slips are empty.

Hundreds of families live and work on Murano, not just in the glass industry but also hired to tend to the hordes of visitors who come to sightsee, eat and drink, and purchase expensive souvenirs. I'm not worried about running into locals. Gianni's factory and showroom are located on the outer tip of the island, where there are no dwellings.

"How do we get inside?" Jerome hisses as we disembark.

"I know where they hide an extra key."

"A key? You haven't been here in—how long? Didn't you say it's been seven years? They must have changed where they hide the key by now, right?"

"If that's the case, then we'll have to find a window I can crawl through."

"No security at all?" he says. "No dogs? Not even a night watchman?"

"What for? Who's going to come all this way to steal a bunch of glass?"

We reach the rear of the factory and two huge arched glass doors covered with wrought iron. I kneel and search along the bottom left panel, which is hollow. I extract the key and hold it up to him. "See?"

"One crime averted," he says as I use the key to open the back door.

We step into a cavernous room filled with furnaces and worktables, lined with shelves of glassblowing tools and accoutrements. I inhale the familiar scent. It's been a long time, but it's as intoxicating as ever. A unique combination of beeswax, paper, and charred cherry wood—all used in different ways during the process of turning lumps of molten lead into glamorous pieces of colored art.

"This way," I say, leading him down a short corridor into a medium-sized room with shelves featuring examples of the most valuable Volpato masterpieces. In the center of the room are four separate stations, each with its own worktable and taboret.

"This is where the designers do the sketching and planning." I point to the one on the far left. "That station was mine." I walk over to sit on the stool. Put my hands on the worn wood surface. It feels as if I never left. The year I became a jewelry designer in my own right, far from my father's oversight. Heady with youth and newfound freedom, inspired by the glories around me, creating glass gems I was so proud of. That same year, I met Hugh and fell in love. I remember it like it was yesterday, and yet it also feels as if it happened to a stranger, not someone I recognize anymore.

I turn on the desk lamp, illuminating the pieces on the shelves behind me.

"What should we be looking for?" Jerome looks around us, confused.

"I don't know," I admit quietly.

He pauses, considering. "Did your father ever visit you here?"

"Just once. He came at the end of my apprenticeship to take me back to New York. It was"—I swallow—"the longest time we'd been apart. But he knows this factory. Gianni and he were—*are*—close friends. He visited here often on his own."

"And he knew this was your workstation?"

I nod. "Yes."

Jerome takes a moment, his brow furrowing before he steps behind me to study the glass vases, goblets, statues, ashtrays, and bowls in the vitrines. Methodically moving from right to left, from one shelf to the next, he examines each piece. It's not until he reaches the last shelf that he lets out an audible breath.

I watch as he fishes into a translucent emerald-colored bowl shaped like petals and pulls it out. Holds the Lemon Twist up to the light, casting reflections about the room.

"I'll be damned," he mutters. He hands the necklace to me. "That was easier than I thought. Now what? I'm having a hard time believing he just left it here for us to find."

"Me, too," I whisper.

Because I already know. But before I can say it, we hear a loud rattle at the showroom door, the clamor of voices outside, shattering the silence as if it too is made of fragile glass.

My father's trap has sprung.

Chapter 15

Jerome

"Get out. Now," I order. She's frozen in place, hesitant, the necklace in her hand like an unwelcome surprise. "Ania, you have to go."

"No," she says. "I can't leave—"

"You have to. The police are here."

Virgil's trap. I understand now, even as the crescendo of angry Italian and tromping footsteps moves toward us. He lured us here to get caught red-handed with the necklace left by *him*. I underestimated him. So did Ania. We'd forgotten what he did to us before in Paris. Chasing us on a motorway and causing a collision that could have killed Luke. We'd unmasked him, thwarted him at his game, forced him to flee into hiding. This is his payback. His gloves are off, as the saying goes. No mercy.

With both of us in jail, he'll be free. No one will ever believe us if we accuse him of being the Leopard.

And he's played us to perfection. Probably sent an anonymous, or not-so-anonymous note to Gabrielli—old friends, after all—expressing concern about the man Ania is keeping company with. Prompted the inquiry into my past, and then the inspector did exactly what I would have done in his shoes: question my suspect enough to push him into making a mistake. To panic at the confiscation of his passport and see where it leads.

"You can't let them catch you," I go on as she stuffs the necklace into her jacket pocket. "There's no evidence if you get away with it."

"They'll still arrest you!"

"Let them. I'll make up an excuse. Get out and wait for me. I'll probably need a lawyer. But they can't find you. You were in the palazzo this entire time. You went to bed early. Jet lag. I took the boat and was gone before you woke up. Ania, there's no time to argue."

She starts to reach for me. I draw away, to her gasp of alarm. Flashlight beams crisscross right outside the room. She bolts away, vanishing seconds before the police crash inside, Gabrielli and a disheveled young man leading the charge.

I assume the young man must be the owner, given his fury. "*Ladro!* In my factory!"

Gabrielli goes still as he sees me with my hands held upright in surrender.

"Signor Curtis." He sighs. "I was hoping it wouldn't be you."

The inspector doesn't say another word as the police handcuff me, and the young man makes a frantic inspection of his premises. Gabrielli then attempts to reassure him, but after being woken up and told that his factory was invaded by an American thief alleged to have stolen a very valuable necklace…not much to say to reassure, is there?

The man barks in English as they take me away, "I'm pressing charges."

Of course, he is.

On the ride back in the police motorboat, Gabrielli looks grim. He has me booked and fingerprinted at the station, then escorted into a sterile, green-painted interrogation room, where I'm left to wait for hours with a lone pack of cigarettes.

A courteous gesture, though I'm cuffed and can't even light one.

When he comes in with a folder, I try not to appear as unsettled as I am.

"This is…unfortunate." He takes a seat opposite me.

I motion to the cigarettes. He sighs and unlocks the cuffs.

"Thanks." My wrists are chaffed. Humiliating enough to be arrested, and I've never been cuffed before. I light up as if it's my last smoke before I'm dragged to a firing squad.

"Why were you in the Volpato factory?" He regards me with a curious mixture of disappointment and suspicion as if the civilized norms that have thus far governed his conduct can—and *will*—be forsaken if I choose to lie to him.

I've had enough time to conceive what I hope is a plausible reason, one Ania can back up if questioned. "A package arrived at the palazzo: a glass statue of a leopard. It made me think I was being framed. I went to check it out."

"A package?" He consults his folder. "Why would you think this? Gianni and Paulo Volpato know Signoria Thorne. She apprenticed with them. Perhaps they sent her a gift."

I cough out a hoarse chuckle. "Of a glass leopard? Pretty strange, don't you think, that the very thing you and I discussed was delivered at the place where I'm staying? Inspector, you implied the Leopard may have been responsible for the theft of the contessa's necklace and the heist in Cannes. That I hadn't done my job investigating. Was I wrong in thinking you suspected I was the thief?"

Gabrielli blinks. "I never said I suspected you of anything, Signor Curtis."

"You didn't have to. When that package arrived—which, by the way, Ania never ordered and was definitely not a gift—I began to think you might not be too far off."

"Oh?" One of his eyebrows arches.

"If it was the Leopard who struck in Cannes and now here, and I was present at both incidents, who better to frame?"

I know I'm treading a very fine line, a narrow filament between truth and falsehood, and he isn't stupid. But if, as I believe, someone alerted him to go to the factory—I'm very sure Ania and I weren't followed; even in the dark and fog, I didn't see or hear any other motorboats and I was looking for them—then it might give him reason for pause. If Virgil identified himself as the worried party, then it could just be paternal concern for his daughter's well-being. If not, well...

Reasonable doubt. It's all I have to work with. Virgil wasn't getting away with this.

The crease on Gabrielli's forehead indicates that he got word, all right. I decide to press my luck. At this point, what do I have to lose?

"Did someone tip you off? Inform you there'd be a break-in at the factory?"

"Signor Curtis." A wry smile. "You know I can't tell you that."

"Well, why else would you have shown up in the dead of night? I got inside without tripping any alarms. No security at all. Very trusting for a world-famous business."

"In Venice, who steals from Murano?" he replies sharply.

"Not me. I wasn't there to steal anything. I mean, think about it. If I'd taken that necklace, why would I steal a bunch of glass?" I ask, recalling Ania's words.

"I do not know." He leans forward. "You tell me."

"I am. I went to check out a hunch. The factory made that sculpture. It had to be a special commission. I was looking for a ledger. A bill of sale. A receipt. Anything to tell me who ordered it made."

"And you thought…forgive me. My English is not so good—"

"Better than my Italian," I cut in.

His frown deepens. "You broke into a factory on Murano because you believed the Leopard was after you? Because a Volpato-made statue was delivered to Signorina Thorne by a family of artisans who have known her and her father for many years?"

"That's right. Look—" I take a moment to appear as if I need to compose myself. He expects befuddlement. Then I hit him with it. "You took my passport. Just mine. I know because I asked Lauren Segal. You came to the palazzo to question me and then showed up at the hotel, to question me again. I might not have been a competent insurance investigator, according to Lambert, but I'm not an idiot. Neither is the Leopard. The new guy in town… Doesn't take a rocket scientist to figure out where this was headed."

"I see." He reclines in his chair. "So, you now believe the Leopard may have stolen from Signorina Thorne in Cannes?"

"It crossed my mind. But I didn't find a glove in Cannes. I had to file my report. After this situation, I started to re-think it. Guess I didn't do such a great job, after all."

"Because…?"

"The contessa's necklace is vintage Thorne. Interesting, yes?" I deliberately echo his manner of speaking. "Investigator. *Commissario*. Very similar. Like the thefts."

He doesn't react visibly, but I sense his discomfort. He's good at his job, takes pride in it, and it's crossed his mind, too. It painted the target on my back.

"Very dramatic," he says at length. "Signorina Segal just gave us a statement that she saw you dancing with the contessa after she spoke with you at the party. She insists you never left the ballroom to go upstairs. She kept her eye on you." Another wry smile, the man of the world. "You have an effect on women, Signor Curtis."

Lauren has come through for me. I owe her one.

"She was flirting with me at the party. She's a very nice girl, but—"

"You're in love with Signorina Thorne. Who can blame you?"

"Ask Ania about the statue. She'll tell you."

"We tried to reach her at the palazzo. She did not answer."

I resist a jolt of fear. "Are you sure? She was asleep when I left."

"No one answered. Perhaps she didn't hear the telephone. We will attempt to contact her in the morning. For now—" He clears his throat. "You are free to go."

"I am?" I didn't expect this. "Really?"

"Signor Volpato wishes to have you charged, but so much paperwork. For what? You broke into his factory with a key left for employees who arrive early. How you knew where the key was is his concern, not mine. If they choose to hide a key where anyone can find it, the police can't be held responsible. You didn't take anything, according to Signor Volpato. A lot of paperwork..." His voice fades to resignation. "You are no thief, Signor Curtis. I cannot speak to your skill as an investigator, but you're a terrible liar."

He stands, picking up the folder. "Perhaps less innocent than you claim, but no thief."

I sag on my chair. I can't believe it.

"Signorina Segal is waiting for you." He pauses at the door. "Sometimes, a nice girl is better than the beautiful one who doesn't answer the telephone when her lover is in jail."

I stumble into dawn breaking over Venice. One night that has felt like years, and I'm disorientated, feeling as if I've been hit by a train.

Lauren stands by a water taxi in her red flannel coat. She turns toward me, relief washing over her face. "Golly. You really know how to stir things up around here."

I crack a smile. "The life of the party, huh?"

"I'll say." She accepts the cigarette I offer. "When the inspector called the hotel, I thought...well, I didn't know what to think. But I came as soon as I could. He asked me a lot of questions about you."

"Yeah, so I gathered." I wince. "The small circle will have a field day with this."

"No." Her voice turns somber. "I won't tell anyone. Promise."

"Thanks." I meet her eyes. "I really didn't expect it to go down this way."

"But you thought something would go down. Didn't you?"

"With Gabrielli hot on my tail and no other suspect? It was obvious."

We smoke in silence. As I crush the butt under my heel, she says, "What now?"

I fish in my pocket to show her my passport. "I'm going to Disneyland."

She laughs. "What about coming to Hollywood, instead?"

A laden silence. Her eyes grow dim.

"Lauren—" I start to say.

"Don't." She cranes on her tiptoes to kiss my cheek. "I get it," she says softly. "She must be something to have you wrapped around her finger. Who knew the Thorne Ice Queen had a heart? Just remember not to be a stranger, okay?" She presses a card into my palm "Call anytime. But don't get arrested again. I'll be in Los Angeles, and it's a long haul to hop a plane to rescue you."

She boards the waiting taxi, waving at me as it draws away.

I watch her disappear down the canal and then call for one myself.

I need to see Ania.

The palazzo is silent. As soon as I enter the foyer, I know. The knowledge seizes my throat until I can barely breathe. I find myself running through the house like a madman, throwing open doors, her name raking talons inside me.

The grey morning drifts over the unmade bed in the master bedroom. The closet doors are open, all her clothing gone. She left in a hurry. Didn't waste any time.

Sometimes, a nice girl is better than the beautiful one who doesn't answer the telephone when her lover is in jail.

I drop to my knees. Bury my face in my hands and choke on despair. Ania, where are you? How am I going to find you?

When I look up, a glitter of something on the bedside table catches the light. I step to it. Incredulous as I gaze at the Lemon Twist. Coiled like a snake, the beautiful yellow stones mocking me with their indifference.

All this over fucking diamonds.

I lunge at it, hurl it across the room with a roar. In the echo of my rage, its shattering against the wall sounds like the air torn apart. Like a rain of shards.

Glass.

My heels crunch on broken bits. I step to where it's sprawled on the floor by the wall where I threw it, cracked into pieces. My heart capsizes in my chest.

It's a fake. An identical glass replica of the necklace we stole.

My father was planning to add a new glass line to our collection… None of this can be a coincidence. My glass line was something he planned to replicate to save himself.

She must have known from the moment I handed it to her in the factory. The lack of weight would have given it away. Glass is lighter than gemstones, and she's a jeweler. She knew and didn't say anything. She left me to get arrested, so she could do…what?

What else? Chase after her father. Hunt down the Leopard. He played us to perfection, with a perfect reproduction, and she's nothing if not his daughter.

She's going after him. She'll never stop until one of them is caught.

And she doesn't want me involved anymore. Too much for me.

Too much for her.

"I will find you," I say into the emptiness. "You can't hide from me, Ania Thorne."

Even if takes my entire life, I'll never stop hunting you, either.

The Heist

By C. W. Gortner and M.J. Rose
Coming August 2, 2022

To catch a leopard wear diamonds.

A year after THE BAIT, Ania Throne is on the prowl. Gone into hiding, she's planned her next move to perfection, intent on winning her dangerous game of cat-against-cat with the Leopard. But Ania doesn't know that even the best-laid heists have hidden flaws.

Jerome Curtis has taken a job at a Hollywood movie studio to try and put his life back together. When a familiar face from the past shows up unexpectedly, Jerome realizes that much as he's tried to forget her, there's no escaping Ania. And this time, what she's about to do could be her doom.

The heist is on. Jerome must join with Ania again to bring down the mastermind thief who's dead-set on not getting caught. Passion and vengeance collide as father and daughter bait each other in a high-stakes gambit, with Jerome caught in the middle. Because no matter how much Ania has tried to keep her lover safe, she's only brought him back into the center of her ploy— and the Leopard intends to take full advantage of it.

From the glamour of late 1950s Hollywood to a desperate chase in the ravines of Los Angeles, two leopards must hunt each other to the end. And only one of them can bring down its prey.

THE HEIST is the thrilling conclusion in the To Catch A Leopard series, a dramatic romantic caper that began with THE STEAL and THE BAIT.

* * * *

1959

There comes a time in life when a man has to admit he has no choice but to cut his losses. I've rarely encountered those times and I'd like to say that when I have, I've been strong enough to admit it. But it hasn't happened very often; it's been a source of pride for me that no matter what was thrown at me, I usually found a way to handle it. Maybe not in the most delicate way, but hey, I'm not a butler. I'm a soldier. I was trained to assess a situation, figure out how much risk it posed to my safety, and then decide the most efficient way to reduce my risk and get the job done.

During the war, I traveled from the chaos of Rome to the sinister grimness of Paris and then through bomb-shattered Germany to the rubble of Berlin. I saw things that few others had, things that still haunt me; and I hunted down the monsters who let it all happen. It wasn't an easy job and it wasn't a pretty one; I made one mistake that I regret. Later on, as an insurance investigator for Lambert Securities, I had to use those same skills to survey a crime scene, figure out who might have stolen the loot and how they did it; and then figure out how to get the loot back before a claim was filed that would cost my employer millions. It wasn't an easy job either, but I can truthfully say that I never made a mistake. The rules for hunting down escaped Nazis are the same rules for catching a thief: assess the risk to your personal safety, the likelihood of surviving the mission, and any weakness that might give you or your opponent an advantage.

It's not pretty, but the rules are simple.

That is, until I got involved with Ania Thorne. And you see, that's when the rules went out the window. She glided into my life with those gorgeous cat-eyes and ballet dancer legs, and she turned me inside out. The rules went by the wayside. Or, if I'm totally honest, I threw them out the window. Because once I had her in my arms, there was no going back to rules. She was playing dirty for keeps and rules weren't her style. It surprised me—and it had been a very long time since anyone had surprised me—and it thrilled me. It also scared the hell out of me. She was way above my league, and I fell hard. Before I even knew it, I was in over my head. Now, it bears asking: how does a guy who hunted war criminals and investigated high-profile thefts get in over his head with a woman?

Well, Ania isn't just any woman. She's a soldier, too, only one who designs very expensive jewelry for a living and has a lot more disposable cash. To catch a leopard, she knew how to bait her trap. When the trap sprang on us instead, she assessed the risks to our personal safety, the likelihood of survival, and any weakness that might give her or our opponent an advantage.

Turns out, I was both the risk and her weakness. So, like any well-trained soldier, she cut her losses. These decisions have to be made to increase the likelihood of survival.

The strangest part is, I get it. I really do. I get why she ditched me. She was way above my league and she has diamond dust in her veins; she understood, like every soldier does, that there comes a time when the mission has come to first.

I get it. That doesn't mean it's pretty or that it makes it any easier.

Because I can't seem to do the same thing to her.

The Steal

By C. W. Gortner and M.J. Rose

They say diamonds are a girl's best friend—until they're stolen.

Ania Throne is devoted to her jewelry company. The daughter of one of the world's most famous jewelers, she arrives in Cannes with a stunning new collection. But a shocking theft by the notorious thief known as the Leopard throws her into upheaval—and plunges her on an unexpected hunt that challenges everything she believes.

Jerome Curtis thinks he's seen it all, especially when it comes to crime. Until he's hired to investigate the loss of Ania Thorne's collection, his every skill put to the test as he chases after a mysterious master-mind responsible for some of the costliest heists in history—and finds himself in a tangled web with a woman he really shouldn't fall in love with.

From the fabled Carlton Hotel to the elegant boulevards of Paris, Ania and Jerome must race against time to catch a thief before the thief catches them. With everything on the line, can they solve the steal or will the steal take more than diamonds from them?

Set in the late 1950s, THE STEAL is a romantic caper by bestselling authors C.W. Gortner and M.J. Rose.

Mademoiselle Chanel
By C.W. Gortner

A stunning novel of iconic fashion designer Coco Chanel—who revolutionized fashion, built an international empire, and become one of the most influential and controversial figures of the twentieth century.

Born into rural poverty, Gabrielle Chanel and her siblings are sent to orphanage after their mother's death. The sisters nurture Gabrielle's exceptional sewing skills, a talent that will propel her into a life far removed from the drudgery of her childhood.

Transforming herself into Coco—a seamstress and sometime torch singer—the petite brunette burns with an incandescent ambition that draws a wealthy gentleman who will become the love of her life. She immerses herself in his world of money and luxury, discovering a freedom that sparks her creativity. But it is only when her lover takes her to Paris that Coco discovers her destiny.

Rejecting the frilly, corseted silhouette of the past, her sleek, minimalist styles reflect the youthful ease and confidence of the 1920s modern woman. As Coco's reputation spreads, her couturier business explodes, taking her into rarefied society circles and bohemian salons. But her fame and fortune cannot save her from heartbreak as the years pass. And when Paris falls to the Nazis, she is forced to make choices that will haunt her.

Mademoiselle Chanel explores the inner world of a woman of staggering ambition whose strength, passion and artistic vision would become her trademark.

The Last Tiara
By M.J. Rose

A provocative and moving story of a young female architect in post-World War II Manhattan who stumbles upon a hidden treasure and begins a journey to discovering her mother's life during the fall of the Romanovs.

Sophia Moon had always been reticent about her life in Russia and when she dies, suspiciously, on a wintry New York evening, Isobelle despairs that her mother's secrets have died with her. But while renovating the apartment they shared, Isobelle discovers something among her mother's effects — a stunning silver tiara, stripped of its jewels.

Isobelle's research into the tiara's provenance draws her closer to her mother's past — including the story of what became of her father back in Russia, a man she has never known. The facts elude her until she meets a young jeweler who wants to help her but is conflicted by his loyalty to the Midas Society, a covert international organization whose mission is to return lost and stolen antiques, jewels, and artwork to their original owners.

Told in alternating points of view, the stories of the two young women unfurl as each struggles to find their way during two separate wars. In 1915, young Sofiya Petrovitch, favorite of the royal household and best friend of Grand Duchess Olga Nikolaevna, tends to wounded soldiers in a makeshift hospital within the grounds of the Winter Palace in St. Petersburg and finds the love of her life. In 1948 New York, Isobelle Moon works to break through the rampant sexism of the age as one of very few women working in a male-dominated profession and discovers far more about love and family than she ever hoped for.

In the two narratives, the secrets of Sofiya's early life are revealed incrementally, even as Isobelle herself works to solve the mystery of the historic Romanov tiara (which is based on an actual Romanov artifact that is, to this day, still missing) and how it is that her mother came to possess it. The two strands play off each other in finely-tuned counterpoint, building to a series of surprising and deeply satisfying revelations.

About C. W. Gortner

C.W. GORTNER holds an MFA in Writing with an emphasis in Renaissance Studies from the New College of California, as well as an AA from the Fashion Institute of Design and Merchandising in San Francisco.

After an eleven year-long career in fashion, C.W. devoted the next twelve years to the public health sector. In 2012, he became a full-time writer following the international success of his novels.

In his extensive travels to research his books, he has danced a galliard at Hampton Court, learned about organic gardening at Chenoceaux, and spent a chilly night in a ruined Spanish castle. His books have garnered widespread acclaim and been translated into twenty-one languages to date. C.W. is also a dedicated advocate for animal rights, in particular companion animal rescue to reduce shelter overcrowding.

Half-Spanish by birth and raised in southern Spain, C.W. lives in Northern California with his husband and two very spoiled rescue cats.

To find out more about his work, visit: http://www.cwgortner.com

About M.J. Rose

New York Times, *USAToday*, and *Wall St. Journal* bestseller, M.J. Rose grew up in New York City mostly in the labyrinthine galleries of the Metropolitan Museum, the dark tunnels and lush gardens of Central Park and reading her mother's favorite books before she was allowed. She believes mystery and magic are all around us but we are too often too busy to notice... books that exaggerate mystery and magic draw attention to it and remind us to look for it and revel in it.

Rose's work has appeared in many magazines including Oprah Magazine and The Adventurine and she has been featured in the New York Times, Newsweek, WSJ, Time, USA Today and on the Today Show, and NPR radio.

Rose graduated from Syracuse University, has a commercial in the Museum of Modern Art in NYC and since 2005 has run the first marketing company for authors - Authorbuzz.com. Rose is also the co-founder of 1001DarkNights.com and TheBlueBoxPress.com

The television series PAST LIFE, was based on Rose's novels in the Reincarnationist series.